"Buffy, there's something you need to know," Giles interrupted in a low voice.

"What?" Buffy asked. "More news flash about what a bad deal Willow is? I got that edition, remember? Read it from cover to cover."

Giles took a deep breath. "Actually, it's about the golem. I think I know who it is."

Buffy stared at him, trying to process this. "Wait—who it is? Since when do men made of dirt actually become someone in particular?"

"Creating a golem takes not only a thorough knowledge of the black arts, which Willow has, but a spirit new to the spiritual realm."

"Well, we certainly lose enough bodies around here on a regular basis," Buffy said. "Who has Willow inserted into tall, dark, and dirty?"

"Riley Finn."

Silence.

Finally Buffy blinked, then frowned at Giles. "Excuse me, I thought you said Riley."

"I did," he said softly.

Buffy swallowed. "But, Giles . . . that would mean he's dead."

Buffy the Vampire Slayer™

Available from SIMON PULSE

Buffy the vampire slayer™

Wicked Willow II

Shattered Twilight

Yvonne Navarro

An original novel based on the hit television series by Joss Whedon

SIMON SPOTLIGHT™

NEW YORK LONDON TORONTO SYDNEY

This book is a work of fiction. Any references to historical events, real people, or real locales are used fictitiously. Other names, characters, places, and incidents are the product of the author's imagination, and any resemblance to actual events or locales or persons, living or dead, is entirely coincidental.

SIMON SPOTLIGHT
An imprint of Simon & Schuster Children's Publishing Division
1230 Avenue of the Americas, New York, New York 10020
™ & © 2004 Twentieth Century Fox Film Corporation. All Rights Reserved.
All rights reserved, including the right of reproduction in whole or in part in any form.
SIMON SPOTLIGHT is a registered trademark of Simon & Schuster, Inc.
The colophon is a trademark of Simon & Schuster.
Manufactured in the United States of America
First Edition 10 9 8 7 6 5 4 3 2 1
Library of Congress Control Number 2003114494
ISBN 0-689-86953-3

For:
Weston.
Yep. Again.

Acknowledgments:

My husband, Weston Ochse
Lisa Clancy
Tricia Boczkowski
Patrick Price
and Gunny Withers,
for letting me have Friday off
(Sorry—no roaming USMC vampires in this one!)

Wicked Willow II

Shattered Twilight

Prologue

"**Y**ou abandoned us."

"Don't be absurd," Willow said. Her back was stiff and straight as she faced Njeri and her coven—or what was left of it. "I did no such thing. If I'd abandoned the coven, none of you would be sitting here now."

Ena, not as strong a Wiccan as Njeri but still high on the power-meter, snorted. "Then let's rephrase. At the very least, I'd say you forget about us," she said in her thick Celtic accent. "It's a bloody miracle you remembered us when you did!"

Willow gritted her teeth. "Again, let me remind you that you wouldn't be here if that were the case."

For a long, uncomfortable minute, no one said anything. Then Sying spoke up, her words tinted with the inflection of her Asian heritage and dripping with acid.

"You sacrificed us to save Buffy Summers. To save the Slayer."

Willow opened her mouth to retort, but nothing would come out. What could she say to that? How could she deny it? It was, at its ugliest, the plain and simple truth.

She had to clear her throat twice before she could speak. "I had my reasons," she finally said in a hoarse voice.

"So you admit it?" Cybele stared hard at her, and Willow had to fight to keep her gaze steady as it met the older woman's. It wasn't the woman's power that bothered her, but the clearness of her eyes, a sort of parental straightforwardness that made little bubbles of guilt form in Willow's throat. "You left us defenseless while you saved the Slayer from a creature we helped you create specifically to gather power for you."

"You weren't defenseless," Willow argued. "You're all very strong and powerful women. You should have banded together to stand up to the spell that Rupert Giles put together. After all, you were only facing two humans and a human-tainted vengeance demon. And the mastermind? A cripple in a wheelchair." She squared her shoulders and sent them all a hard look. "I still find it hard to believe you couldn't take them on— that you let them finish the spell and overwhelm you."

"We did a passable job of stalling the start of the spell," Njeri said defensively. "No thanks to you."

"You should have been able to do better than that," Willow shot back. "It should have been *easy* for you to stop it, been something you barely thought about. Better than that, it should have been easy for you to destroy the three who broke in here, to step on them like bugs."

"Excuse me," Ena said, "but I didn't know we *had* to." She waved a hand at the loft, which was considerably more bare than it had been, now that Giles's relocation spell had emptied it of everything small and moveable. "Since you made it clear that we had no choice about being here, I assumed we were under your protection."

"Well, you know the old cliché about assuming," Willow said, but she sounded a lot more flippant than she felt. She wasn't pleased at being put on the defensive. While she wasn't afraid of these women, even en masse, five were already gone and she did *not* want to lose any more of them.

Was it her fault?

Without a doubt . . . yes.

Standing here, being judged by the seven remaining members of her once-strong coven, the memory of a couple of nights ago came back to her full force, as did the choices she had made. Yes, she had sacrificed part of her coven to save Buffy's life, but it hadn't been willingly. It had been because of the Ghost of Tara, who had been with her twenty-four/seven since a short time after the death of her physical body. Tara's spirit had been the driving force, that one thing underneath everything that made Willow do the things—*all* the things—that she now did.

Willow's gaze touched on each of them, and she couldn't help remember when they had numbered twelve, and had been complete, and so very much stronger. She had wanted power, more and more of it, to help her gather the strength she would need to resurrect Tara. She still needed that power, but wisdom dictated she go about getting it in more careful ways. Her last attempt, when she and the coven had created a blue cat-demon called a *sine kot diabl*, had ended up out of control. The creature was supposed to go out each night and feed only on dark-minded beings like itself, then return before each dawn to purge its power resources into Willow. At the end, it had refused to turn over the power it collected and, despite repeatedly being commanded not to do so, it had attacked Spike. Both Spike and Oz had been helpless, to a point, since Willow had deemed both her personal pets—after putting a perpetual werewolf spell on Oz—and chained them to either side of the fireplace with unbreakable magic bonds.

Willow and the *sine kot diabl* had ended up locked in battle on the street below her loft, and when Buffy had shown up, the Slayer hadn't been able to see the cat-demon and hadn't understood what Willow was fighting. But the *sine kot diabl*, though invisible to Buffy because she was essentially good, still apparently sensed some darker essence in Buffy herself, perhaps that long-ago original source of her power that some believed to have come from a demon. When the *sine kot diabl* had attacked Buffy, Willow had shrugged and stepped aside, content to stand by and watch her former friend turned nemesis finally come to an end. As it was happening, she'd realized that Giles, that meddlesome former Watcher whom she'd crippled in a devastating battle at the Magic Box, had started a spell to destroy her coven. She'd started to go up and stop it—

And the Ghost of Tara had intervened.

Why had she listened?

Willow wasn't sure. At that point it hadn't yet become a forced thing, an issue of choosing between one or the other. But Willow had been torn by things the Ghost of Tara had reminded her about, things like how many times Buffy had put Willow's safety before hers and how many times she had chosen to give something up in order to either keep Willow safe or outright save her life. In the end Willow had just had a good old overdose of the personal guilt thing. She'd buried her hands in the *sine kot diabl*'s skull and crushed the life—and her conduit to Sunnydale's untapped power—right out of it.

Too late she realized the damage that Giles's spell was doing up there in her loft. She'd done what the Ghost of Tara had asked, and it was not her job to see that Buffy recovered—she would live or she wouldn't. She'd risen through the window of her loft to discover her place in chaos, most of the smaller furniture and precious spell books gone, as were the majority of her magicks items, the trinkets and potions and lighter stones. Worse, five of her Wiccans were also gone, sucked through a transportational portal created by Giles's spell, whisked away to locales unknown and unreachable. Now, no matter what she tried, Willow could not find them, and whether they would ever make their own way back to Sunnydale (if they even wanted to, given the way she had "urged" them to help her) was a question that only time—long periods of it—would answer.

It had taken two Wiccan demands before the spell shut down, and then she'd been faced with the tools that Rupert Giles, a defeated man she'd condemned to a wheelchair, had used to bring destruction down upon her carefully chosen twelve: Anya, Xander, and Dawn.

Her vengeance would have been great, indeed. Only Warren would have known a harder death, but for one simple thing that had intervened: the Ghost of Tara.

"If you kill them, I will leave you."

Every time she replayed those words in her mind, they cut through Willow's heart—still burned as though she were hearing them for the first time. She would live without Tara's physical presence and body—for now—because she must.

But Willow would not do something to drive away Tara's spirit, the last remaining fragment of her lover that she had.

As if she knew the direction Willow's thoughts had taken, Njeri's voice rose over Cybele's, her words harsh. "To make it even worse, you let the three who did the spell go free," she said accusingly. "You didn't even avenge us." She jerked her head toward where the Ghost of Tara stood off to the side, standing silent and forever covered in the blood evidence of her death. "Instead you let that ghost tell you what to do."

"The spirit controls you like a puppet," Ena said derisively. "She says jump, you say how many times."

Willow flushed. "Leave the Ghost of Tara out of this," she snapped. "I make my own choices."

"Yes," Cybele said, and raised one finely groomed eyebrow. "But how wise are they? You let a spiritual entity dictate your actions—an entity you plan to bring back to physical form. So what if she *does* make good on her threat to leave? She will return anyway when you force her back into existence." She looked confidently at the other Wiccans. "She will have no choice."

"I need her here with me now," Willow said stiffly.

"Why?" asked Ellen. Blond and blue-eyed, she looked deceptively sweet and innocent, like Willow's high school classmate Harmony had when she'd been human; now Harmony was a vampire who went along placidly on the surface but would, like just about any other vampire, turn and kill at a moment's notice. "I'm no psychologist, but it doesn't take a degree to know that having her around all the time is pure torture. She's nothing but a distraction, Willow. You should have let her go and saved the other five."

"Enough!" Willow cried. "Things are what they are!"

"That's what I've been telling you all along, my love."

Willow barely stopped herself from jumping at the sudden ghostly voice, then balled her fist when one of the usually more quiet Wiccans rolled her eyes at the Ghost of Tara's unexpected words. Her eyes blazed, and when Ellen realized she'd been caught, she froze like a rabbit in the headlights of a truck. "Do not mock me, Ellen," Willow said in a low, dangerous voice. "Do not *ever* make fun of me."

"I-I'm sorry," Ellen stammered. "That was f-foolish. I didn't mean—"

"Yes, it was." Willow's voice echoed around the other Wiccans and they glanced at one another nervously. There was a tone in Willow's voice, a strange, vague . . . echo, that said she'd been pushed just the other side of too far. Abruptly, the high ceiling in the loft seemed even higher than it had been before; now it was cloaked in darkness and a layer of hazy, smoke-colored clouds, like Willow's anger made manifest. "What you didn't *mean* was to get caught." For a moment, she almost let her anger take her, and in so doing, nearly allowed her rage to consume them, too.

But . . . no.

Willow inhaled deeply, concentrating on the oxygen filling her lungs, feeling it disperse throughout her body—into her bloodstream and brain, her pores, her taste buds—filling everything with calmness, a sense of blue cool that stilled, at least for the moment, the furious fires that threatened to destroy those around her. And why?

Because of Tara, of course.

She knew it, they knew it, the Ghost of Tara knew it. If the spirit disapproved of what she did, she might threaten to leave again, as she had when Willow had prepared to deal the killing blow to Anya, Xander, and Dawn for carrying out the spell that had fragmented her coven. Who were these women to make fun of her, to look down their noses and sneer, when they had never experienced the sort of loss that Willow had? Yet that was it exactly: They simply didn't *know*. Tara had been the second half of not just Willow's heart, but her *soul*, and there wasn't another person in this oversized room who could understand the level of need that Willow carried within her.

Sometimes a simple admission of guilt earned a person more respect than did a dozen excuses.

"I'm sorry," Willow said. "You're right. You're *all* right. I did what I had to in order to keep the Ghost of Tara with me. And I'd do it again. There's no sense lying about it. Tara is the reason you're all here, the reason I'm gathering power. She is everything to me—more than any of you or all of you put together." Willow raised her chin. "If that sounds uncaring, it's not meant to. It's just a bald fact. What I *can* promise is that I won't make the same mistake twice. Now that I know that Rupert Giles's goal is to break us apart, I'll never let him or anything else sidetrack me enough to leave you unprotected again."

"Really." It was impossible to miss the suspicion in Njeri's voice. "And what if the Ghost of Tara comes between you and us another time? What then?"

What if, indeed?

Willow found she couldn't meet the dark gaze of the other Wiccan. "I will find a way to keep the balance," she vowed. "I swear, I *will*." She looked around at all of them. "That's the best I can promise," she said.

No one spoke, until finally Cybele cleared her throat. "Then I suppose it will have to be enough," the older woman said calmly. "We have all had to make difficult choices at different times in our lives. Let's hope that Willow never has to make another one such as this, or better yet, that she takes whatever steps are necessary to ensure that she's never put in such a position again." She pressed her lips together and looked at Willow solemnly. "Or that we are, either."

Well aware that she had just been chastised by her own coven, Willow nodded as regally as she could. Humiliation warred with practicality, what she'd really wanted to do was throw a good old-fashioned Wiccan temper tantrum—bounce a few of them off the ceiling and floor like Ping-Pong balls, spin them around like tops, hang them up like sides of beef from invisible hooks. But that would only serve to alienate them even more, and while she was fully capable of forcing them to work for her, it would take far less energy if they did so more or less willingly.

"Rupert Giles will not give up," Willow said, as much to divert their attention from her as remind them that the danger had not at all passed. "He's part of Buffy's little pack of nonstop do-gooders, and they never want to see any kind of power in any one person's hands, particularly if that person doesn't happen to be under their control."

Ena's eyes flashed with the challenge. "So we can expect more of the same, eh?" There was no missing the anticipation in her voice. "Well, he's unlikely to catch us so much by surprise in a second go 'round!"

"You can say that again," Kala muttered. "I never did like surprises, even when I was a kid. When I was a sophomore in high school back in Baltimore, a bunch of girls thought they were going to put me through some stupid 'new-girl initiation' ritual. Tried to lock me in the basement with the rats and the creepy old custodian." She grinned in pleasure at the memory. "I turned him into a rat and gave the four girls a case of permanent pubescent acne."

The other women around the room chuckled, but Kala's words had sparked a memory in Willow's head. Now she stood and gestured at the rest of them. "All of you, go home and get some rest. Meet me back here tomorrow night and I will have our numbers once again returned to thirteen strong." She smiled confidently. "I promise you, there are still many strong and beautiful Wiccans to be found, right here in our hometown of lovely little Sunnydale, U.S. of A."

Chapter One

Okay, Buffy thought. *So maybe this wasn't the best idea I've ever had.*

The bigger question: Was she talking about her not-so-new job or going out to patrol right after her four A.M. shift ended?

"I never had a Slayer soda before," the vampire in front of her said. "Though I hear you girls taste real good. Exotic—not like normal folks." A skinny, dorky looking guy, he looked like he'd have a hard time killing a big cockroach. To top it off, he had this nasal, whiny voice that made him sound like he was talking with big wads of cotton stuffed up his nose. Then again, Buffy had learned many, *many* times that looks could be devastatingly deceiving. He grinned, showing the expected sharp-tipped teeth, except they had big gaps in between them. All he needed was a plaid flannel shirt and a long, fuzzy-ended weed sticking out of one corner of his mouth. Where'd this guy come from, anyway, an out of the way Louisiana swamp? And if so, how the heck had he found his way to Sunnydale?

"One time I talked to this guy," Whiny Voice continued, "and he was telling me how he killed two Slayers, how he's the only one who's ever done that." He grinned nastily. "I figure taking you down gets me halfway to the record."

Rankled by the reference to Spike, Buffy started to retort, but another vampire spoke up before she could, strutting a little as he stepped forward.

"Hey," protested one of Whiny's companions, "you ain't the only one here, remember? You can't take credit for the kill when it's gonna be all of us pitching in to make it happen." If it hadn't been for the scrunched-up vampire face, this guy might have actually looked normal.

The first vampire frowned. "Well, it's not like she's going to stand a chance against all five of us."

"Yeah, but fair's fair," said another, this one a blond-headed teenager wearing a black T-shirt with the word *Preppies* inside a circle with a slash across it. His short hair was spiked and he had earrings in both ears. "We should all have a share."

"Oh, we'll have a share, all right." The second bloodsucker licked his lips and leered at Buffy. "She's kind of small, but she'll make a good shared *snack*."

"Well, I want first bite," insisted Whiny Voice. "I'm the one who found her."

"Who made you leader?" demanded the teenager. "You're always horning in on stuff, taking first dibs when you have no right. I say we draw straws for her or something. There's gotta be a fair way to decide."

"Yoo-hoo," Buffy said loudly, waving her arms to get their attention. "Remember me? The Slayer who's standing here bored as you discuss me like I'm the last frozen turkey on the eve of Thanksgiving?" They all stared at her openmouthed. For crying out loud, they really *had* forgotten about her, or at least that she was still conscious and ready to kick. She shook her head in disgust. "I'm sorry, but no one *asked* me if I was still cooking." She gave them a wry smile. "I'm definitely still cooking!"

And she let herself go on autopilot.

Real-life fights were never like the movies. Buffy always got a charge out of watching them go down on the big screen or on television, but please—when was the last time anyone stood by and patiently waited their turn to attack while the fellow in front of them got trounced or dusted? Not likely. In reality, one or two might hang back, not wanting to get whacked by the flying fists or painful kicks meted out by the other combatants, friend or foe, content to watch and wait. Like now, where four of the five vampires made a nearly simultaneous grab for her, although Buffy made it a point to be nowhere near where they thought she should be. Witness precisely why they *ought* to have hung back and assessed the situation: the bunch of them got all tangled up with the others' hands and Buffy even thought she heard a few heads knock together amid the yelps of "Ow!" and "Hey, watch it!"

Buffy spun, knowing better than to let the four of them come after her unprotected back. If she hadn't been thinking so much about Willow, and Giles's failed attempt at dispersing her coven, she would have realized that these jerks had her pegged for a post-closing breakfast, and had probably been monitoring her all night long. Ever since the thorough pounding she'd taken by that invisible-cat thingy that Willow had created, the patrons at the bar had been giving her an increasingly difficult time. The clientele had never been yuppie polite—it just wasn't that kind of place—but at least before they'd shown her a modicum of respect. But that was back then, when she'd started as a cocktail waitress and then whaled the fire out of three bikers when their leader had pinched her on the butt—and this was now. It was a pretty good bet that—

"Word gets around, you know." Whiny Voice had extricated himself from his buddies and was again advancing on her. "The whole town's heard about how you been getting your backside regularly kicked by the new witch on the block. And let's not forget that you nearly got sent to deaddom by"—he snickered—"a big blue *cat*."

"Too bad the thing's not around to check you out," Buffy shot back. "It seemed to have a preferred taste for night scum like you and your friends."

The vampire shrugged and acted like he was going to reply, then he leaped on her.

But Buffy was ready. She'd let them all think she was focused on bickering, when in reality she was well aware that the other four were trying to surreptitiously circle around behind her. When Whiny Voice would have grabbed her, Buffy neatly sidestepped to her left; as he stumbled where she was, she cupped her right hand behind his skull and used her left to grab the back waistband of his jeans. A nice hard twirl, and suddenly she held a demon wrecking ball; Whiny Voice unwillingly bowled down the other three attackers with barely any effort at all on Buffy's part.

"Enough of this playing around," she said to no one in particular. Still spinning, she let go of the bloodsucker's head and pulled back with her left hand while her right slipped into her back pocket. The vampire jerked upright, then bawled as she shoved him forward again, this time toward the waiting stake.

One down, three to go.

Wait—

Make that four.

The other three were clambering to their feet, eyeing her warily, seeing and instantly forgetting the remains of their dead comrade with the customary lack of concern that most vampires had for one another. That fifth guy, though . . . he was creepy. He had held back, kept himself apart from the general punchfest. He was *still* hanging back, but somehow Buffy was certain it wasn't because of cowardice. Oh no, this one was deliberately observing, learning, taking it all in. It was always the quiet ones you had to watch out for.

"So I guess that taking out one of us makes you think you're tough," said the spiky-haired teen. "You got a long ways to go."

Buffy shrugged. "Maybe . . . but maybe not. Of course, three against one is the coward's way to fly, but hey, you probably need all the help you can get."

The young vampire's face twisted in anger at the insult. "Hey, I don't need no—"

"Don't listen to her, Mike," one of the other two said hastily. So Buffy finally had a name for the youngest of the crew. "She's just talking trash, trying to get you to come at her without any help." He put a hand on Mike's arm, but Mike just shook it off.

So much for the vampire's attempt at wisdom. "I don't need any help with her," Mike snapped. "She's just a girl and Jesse was stupid and careless. I can handle this one just fine by myself."

Jesse—that must have been Whiny Voice's real name. "Oh, definitely," Buffy said. "I'm just a girl. You can beat me easily." She batted her eyelashes at him mockingly.

"Mike—"

"Shut up," he said grimly, "and stay the hell out of it, too. No blondie bimbo's gonna get away with making fun of me."

He charged her, and Buffy did have to give him a little credit for speed; it must have been his youth that gave him that, because it sure didn't give him any experience. He covered the ground between himself and Buffy in hardly any time at all, but the two rapid punches he threw at her were still nothing but haymakers, the kind a drunk in a bar might throw. You practically had a week to duck under the coming fist. She went under the first and to the inside so that the second swung at nothing; Mike stared at it stupidly for about one second too long.

A not-so-regrettably short-lived walk on the dark side of existence.

The other two were nearly as boastful and lacking in brains. They attacked her together, and finally, *finally*, Buffy had a little bit of pizzazz to wake her from the doze she was starting to worry would lull her to sleep. A punch here, a backfist there, half a dozen rapid roundhouse kicks, and three minutes later—the length of a good boxing round—the score was in Buffy's favor. When it came right down to it, four dusters in one night was a pretty good tally.

Ah, but then there was number five.

Standing silently, waiting and watching. Buffy peered at him suspiciously, but there was something about him that quieted her tendencies to be sarcastic, something dark and dangerous that reminded her, perhaps, of a lizard. Or maybe a dragon.

He'd been smoking, and now he dropped his cigarette butt to the concrete and ground it out with the heel of his shoe. Dressed all in black, his confident movements and outfit reminded her of Spike—that is if Spike dyed his hair jet black to match his clothes. When the remaining vampire raised his head and regarded her, Buffy realized he was Asian, although she wasn't up on her anthropology enough to be able to tell much more than that. What was up, *high* up, was instinct, and everything inside her was telling her that this man was skyscrapers above her earlier casualties in both methods and skill.

Still not speaking, he stepped forward, moving with the fluidity of a snake. He stopped when he was still out of convenient attacking range, like a predator deciding which way is the best way to take down the coming kill. Rather than waste her breath, Buffy waited with him, giving him as much as he gave on the silent treatment front. After a few long and rather nerve-wracking moments, her new opponent slid one well-manicured hand inside his jacket.

Buffy tensed. Maybe time would dull the memory, but for now she couldn't help associate a move like that with Warren and the gun, even if the trauma of him shooting her had wiped the actual memory from her mind. But no, this man would not use such an unrefined weapon. When he pulled his hand free, Buffy saw the weapon held in his relaxed and confident grip. For a moment it didn't register—she couldn't recall ever having faced such a thing.

A whip.

Crap, Buffy thought, and then she didn't have time to think about anything but getting the hell out of the way.

Later, she would realize that part of the problem was the unnerving resemblance that the sound of a cracking whip—at least this one—had to a gunshot. It worked on her subconscious, reminding her with every *craaaaaack!* of that fateful day in the yard. Slayer speed and slayer reflexes saved her now—at least most of the time—and the few times she actually *did* get stung made her cry out in pain and empathy for those pour souls whom she'd read about in history, the ones who'd suffered forty or fifty or—God forbid—a hundred lashes for some imagined infraction against their cruel master.

Her opponent attacked again, his movements like quicksilver. The leather bit into her flesh, this time wrapping around her left forearm like a coil of fire. Buffy bit her lip against the pain and tasted blood, but that didn't stop her from wrapping her right hand around the disgustingly warm ribbon of leather and tugging it with all her strength. It pulled free and suddenly she had the vampire's weapon, even if it was still entwined around her skin tightly enough to sink into—

Craaaaaaack!

A snap of agony caught her fully across one cheek and Buffy howled with pain and went down. She should have considered this, should have realized that someone so deadly and smart, so *cunning,* would never rely on just one weapon. She hit the ground painfully and rolled, and he missed with his next blow—barely. Still, there was no getting away from the torturous welt he'd put across her face, and the pain was a terrible thing, big enough to nearly eclipse rational thought. He followed with his second whip, pulling it back and sending snapping attacks at her one after another. Sidewalk pebbles and dirt scratched Buffy's clothes and skin as she kept turning on the ground, but she didn't care, didn't feel anything but the flames eating into her cheek. She finally got her other hand around the elaborately carved handle of the first whip and managed to unwind it as she went. One more roll—

—and she met the next heavy crack of the vampire's second whip with the leather of the first one stretched firmly out to trap it.

His blow tied up one strip of leather with the other, winding it far too tightly for him to pull it free. Moving on motion memory and training, Buffy's attacker grunted in surprise when his tug jerked him up short. He pulled back on the whip instinctively, and when it didn't release, he dropped the handle. Who knows what he would have done then—maybe reached inside his coat and come up with yet another whip, or something worse—but by now Buffy had a trusty Mr. Pointy out and hurling through the air, straight at his chest. He didn't have enough time to dodge the piece of wood completely, but as every good martial artist is taught, the opponent's blow doesn't have to miss by a mile. An inch or so to one side or another can mean all the difference in the world.

The dark-haired vampire hissed in pain, then gripped the shaft of the stake and yanked it from the meaty part of his upper left shoulder. Blood, black-looking in the wan light of an overhead street lamp, pulsed sluggishly from the wound, leaving an ugly, oily-looking stain on the front of his black jacket. His calculating eyes, black like the rest of him, glittered with hatred as his gaze fixed on Buffy.

"A victory for you tonight, Slayer." Despite the pain he *had* to be enduring, the vampire's tone was evenly modulated and he inclined his head respectfully in Buffy's direction. "But we *will* meet again."

Buffy clawed at the leather encircling her left arm and finally got it free. "I'll be sure to practice my aim."

But the nameless vampire was gone, melted into the darkness like night fog dissipating in the early light of dawn.

Chapter Two

She'd sent the other members of her coven home, and now the loft was quiet and soaked in premorning dimness. Spike and Oz were asleep, the vampire cloaked in dreams of personal madness, the werewolf cradled by his own unconcerned savagery. Every now and then the drafts would carry one of Spike's sleep-drenched sobs to Willow's ears, and each time that happened, Oz would automatically growl, as though he were some kind of supernatural guard dog watching over a private land of nightmares. Willow thought that notion might be close to the truth, although it was doubtful she would ever know for sure.

After everyone had left, she'd cleared the top of her largest table; already new potions, spell books, and dozens of assorted trinkets had been restocked in the loft to take the place of the items sucked through the portal Giles had created. Now Willow carefully spread a map of the world on the cleared space, smoothing it at the edges while at the same time being careful not to tear the fragile parchment at its fold lines. This wasn't a map that a person could check out from the Sunnydale Public Library for a couple of weeks while they did a world history paper. Oh no; if someone, Giles perhaps, had maintained a list of documents important in the realm of the supernatural—and let's face it, Willow figured the former librarian probably did just that—this fractured and old graph would probably be in the top ten.

She ran her fingertips lightly over the map's surface, wishing it could show her more than it did. All the countries of the world were there, including shifts in cartography as recent as yesterday—it was just that kind of magickal chronicle. All the lines were handdrawn, and as she studied it, Willow swore she could literally *see* them shifting at the borders between warring Middle Eastern countries. It was an ever-changing world.

From an adjacent shelf, Willow gathered up the things she would need: a pinch of sand from the hot desert, a tiny vial of melted snow harvested from the top of a lofty overseas mountain, the rich, dried remains of a once deep green leaf plucked from a fig tree, the ground-up pit from an imported olive, a sprinkle of special sea salt found only along the Irish coast, and more. When she had collected over twenty items, Willow mixed them one at a time into a wide, handmade stoneware bowl decorated with ancient, little-known symbols around its rim. She smiled with satisfaction as the special combination of dry ingredients made the inside surface of the pottery start to glow a deep orange. Yes, it looked like her spell was already well on its way to working.

"The world is made of water and land," she murmured softly as she passed her hand back and forth over the bowl. "Plants and earth, rock and man." She reached over and picked up a small bottle of ocean water, then pulled the cork and held it over the bowl. "Drink of this water to be complete, to tell me where my witches keep." With that she dribbled the water in a steady, counter-clockwise motion across the surface of the bowl's contents.

The mass in the bowl soaked up the seawater, then began to bubble thickly, glowing intensely with heat and spitting in the air like hot lava. Willow paid it no mind; instead she thrust her bare fingers into the bowl and scooped up a palm full of the stuff. Then, in one hard sweeping motion, she hurled it across the surface of the ancient map.

None of it touched the map's surface. Most of it rolled uselessly off the side of the ancient paper and onto the table. But three small lumps stopped, suspended in the air above the map as though lying on an invisible glass surface. After a second's pause, each one burst into flame, then drew down until they burned like tiny, persistent candles.

"There," Willow said. Now *this* was measurable progress—each flame represented the location of one of the Wiccans whom Giles had sent into the wild black yonder. "Three out of five isn't bad." Actually she was quite happy—a part of her had been secretly afraid that Giles had banished her Wiccans to one or more totally different dimensions. That would have made it a lot harder for her to find them. Of course, five out of five would have been better, but sometimes a person just has to be happy with what they could get. Even so, it was just too bad the map wouldn't locate Jonathan and Andrew for her; then again, they were just dweebs—*guilty* dweebs, but still—and thus they had no true power for the spell to track.

Without warning, the Ghost of Tara was at her side. *"I've said exactly that to you on several occasions. It goes hand in hand with the old saying about leaving well enough alone."*

Willow was not surprised that the spirit would show up to comment on what she was doing. The Ghost of Tara had been with her almost from the moment Willow had first finished outfitting this loft as her new place to live and work, always ready to throw an opinion or two into the mix. Despite the fact that the Ghost of Tara almost always seemed to disapprove of her actions, Willow had never lost the desire to have her there. And in that same vein—

"I think I can say with all honesty that I've done just that with your death," she said calmly. She risked a glance at the Ghost of Tara, then wished she hadn't. Where was it written that spirits weren't allowed to change their clothes? Next to having Tara physically come back, Willow would have given almost anything to be able to see Tara wearing something other than the blood-stained blouse in which she had been murdered. It was a repeated stab to Willow's heart, a constant reminder that she had been thus far unable to realize her goal of finalizing the proper spell to resurrect her dead lover.

"And yet that is also something you refuse to let be." The Ghost of Tara stared at her sadly and Willow ached to touch the golden blond hair framing the face just inches away from her own. But there was no sense even trying—her hand would go right through the specter and she would only be more frustrated for having tried.

"Haven't we had this conversation before?" Willow asked without any true impatience. "Wait—that's right. The last time was already a few hours ago, so it must be time for a retake, just in case I've forgotten."

"I am only trying to make you see that you will never succeed," the Ghost of Tara said gently. *"I cannot bear to know that you will be disappointed."*

"Can you see the future, Tara?" Not wanting to meet the Ghost of Tara's gaze, Willow kept staring at the small flames burning above the map on the table. "Now that you're dead, do you actually *have* that power?"

"No," the spirit admitted. *"No, I don't."*

"Then you can't say for sure that I'll fail," Willow said with finality. "And so you will *never* convince me not to try."

"I will not give up."

Willow nodded. She could accept this. After all, she wasn't going to give up either.

Rather than continue the discussion—she refused to call these "arguments"—Willow turned back to the spell she was putting together. She was halfway there, but the second part was what really counted. From one of the work shelves behind her, she pulled another earthenware bowl she'd prepared a little earlier. This bowl was much the same as the first, except its contents were far simpler and quite easy to procure: nothing but rich and ultra-basic Sunnydale, California, soil. Yep—all-American home.

A quick glance told her that the Ghost of Tara had wandered elsewhere, this time over to Oz. She liked to stand over there sometimes, and apparently the man-turned-into-perpetual-werewolf found her presence comforting, even though the beast didn't seem able to quite focus on exactly what was in front of him. Sometimes Willow would watch as the Ghost of Tara ran her fingers across the top of Oz's fur-covered scalp, neck, and back; lately, though, Willow had started turning away at the sight. She didn't know if it was really true, but the idea that the werebeast might be able to feel the touch of Tara's spirit while she herself could not made her blackly jealous.

She dug both hands into the bowl of Sunnydale earth, enjoying the gritty feeling of the moist soil between her fingers. Quickly, as though she were a child making mud pies, she fashioned three small balls of earth, each no bigger than a golf ball. As she dropped them one by one into the pseudo-lava floating in the other bowl, she began to chant. Her voice was strong and clear as it carried across the expanse of the loft, making both Oz and Spike break from their slumber and look in her direction.

"Loki, hear my command and heed my direction." With her hands still covered in the grime from the earth-filled bowl, Willow dug again into the bubbling red liquid and found the three earthen balls. She held them up until the excess fiery-looking goo sloughed away, and they looked like three miniature coals pulsing within her cupped palms.

Suddenly the Ghost of Tara was once more at her side. *"Beware, Willow. Loki is cunning and a trickster. He will delight in providing not what you see, but what you think you do. You may regret demanding his assistance."*

Willow felt a muscle tick in her jaw, but she would not break her concentration. She loved Tara above all things, but the spirit side of her was even more suspicious and a doomsayer than the physical had been. "Seek the bearers of the power to which I send you, and return them to me now!" She spread her fingers and let the mini balls of false fire drop into the bowl of Sunnydale earth. They rolled there and stopped, coated in earthlike balls of pseudochocolate cookie dough.

Often her spells had a lag time, a few seconds in which she could start forming the first shreds of doubt about whether the incantation had been successful. Not this one—amidst a background of abrupt, booming laughter, there were three brilliant flashes of reddish-orange light. Willow automatically shielded her eyes; as she did so, the laughter swelled and expanded to a nearly hysterical level. It didn't sound at all funny, and

Willow was just about to fire out a few words in Latin to make it stop when it ended of its own accord. In the sudden and rather shocking silence that followed, she got a really good look at the three Wiccans her spell had found and returned to her.

They all lay together in a crumpled heap in the center of the loft's floor. Below them the once golden wood was now dark and filthy, smeared with blood and the black smudges of other . . . *matter*, quite pungent, that Willow didn't care to identify. While they hadn't been gone that long, it was painfully obvious that a lot could happen in a very little time. All three were ragged and filthy, and not one looked as though she'd fared very well. Two of them, Anan and Chiwa, were climbing to their feet, already looking around with relief and ready for recovery.

The third, Flo, was a slobbering, snapping mass of complete insanity.

She had once been a pretty young woman. Maybe not beautiful, but her hair had been a lovely chestnut brown, shining and halfway down her back. Hazel eyes, and regal, rather chiseled features topped a nearly six-feet-tall frame that had made her look a little haughty, proud even though her power level wasn't all that high on the Wiccan scale. Willow wasn't precisely sure where Flo had ended up; she doubted that Giles, in his infinite lack of foresight and wisdom, had even considered that aspect. On the map, Flo's little flame had hovered somewhere around Thailand; the way the markings in that area had been hand-drawn and sur- rounded by dark art symbols made it impossible to tie the flame into a solid, modern-day location. But wherever she'd been, Flo had clearly been existing in a living hell . . . and obviously she still thought she was there.

Her hair was so tangled and woven with strange things that it looked like some kind of tortured bird's nest. It was full of . . . stuff—bits and pieces that might have been fabric and dead leaves, pieces of leather and lengths of twisted, coat hanger-like metal. Worse than that, Willow could have sworn that even from her position a good twenty feet away, she could see shapes in it, small things moving around within that tangled mass of hair and other unidentifiable objects.

It took hardly any time at all for Anan and Chiwa to register Flo's condition and instinctively scramble away. They were in considerably better shape, although Willow thought it was damn clear that they hadn't been exactly traveling on a nice, fattening vacation cruise. In just the few days that they'd been gone, each had lost a good five to ten pounds—severe stress could do that—and now they were leaner and meaner, in both physical appearance and in the soul-view of their gaze, which was hooded and dark, darting in all directions as if something might leap out of the corners toward them at any moment. It wasn't a pretty thing to view, and it made Willow silently curse that meddlesome former Watcher. She really should have killed him when she'd had the chance.

Flo's guttural snarl jerked Willow back to the present. A formerly weak Wiccan she might have been, but there was nothing wimpy about the sounds coming out of Flo's mouth now, nor the ferocious way she was staring at Oz. Willow had just enough time to register this before Flo leaped.

She barely got her hand up in time to stop Flo's attack. A painful flash of light knocked Flo to the floor, and before she could get up and try again, Willow mumbled a few words and wrapped her tightly in a binding rope of blue light. While blue was supposed to be the great color of calmness, it did little to soothe the returned Wiccan; Flo writhed ceaselessly on the floor, howling like a banshee the entire time.

"*Well,*" said the Ghost of Tara, "*I see Loki granted your wish. Your charges were returned to you . . . though obviously not in the same condition as they were when they were taken.*" When she spoke, Willow could hear her words clearly, despite Flo's wailing. "*I warned you that he would betray you, just as I told you about the* sine kot diabl. *Why don't you ever listen to me?*"

Willow hissed air through her teeth. It was true that the Ghost of Tara had warned her about Loki, and yes, she should have known he would find a way to screw things up. He was just like the devil in all those old pulp movies and books, always finding a way to turn some hapless person's deal with the devil into a curse. But darn it, she needed these Wiccans back here and she would reclaim them no matter what. Despite what she'd told the members of her coven earlier, strong Wiccans, the really good ones, weren't exactly falling out of trees here in Sunnydale. For overpopulation, a person really had to look to the vamps, with the demons running a not-so-close second.

"Maybe," Willow said as she watched Flo and wondered what the hell to do about her, "it's because although I *know* you're Tara, you don't . . . talk to me like Tara did. You're so *stiff*, so . . . formal. It's like someone took a metal rod and sewed it inside your back and now it hurts you all the time or something. You never soften up. You never . . . laugh." Willow finally looked unhappily at the Ghost of Tara. "You're Tara, but at the same time, you're not."

The Ghost of Tara regarded her. *"Being dead takes all the humor out of existence on this plain,"* the spirit said solemnly. *"Humor, laughter, love—all that—goes hand in hand with life. I no longer* have *life."*

"So this means what?" Willow stared at her. She was almost too afraid to ask her next questions. "That you don't love anymore? That you don't love *me*?"

"Of course I do," the Ghost of Tara said. *"I will always love you. It's just that love . . ."* She hesitated. *"It changes with the dying of the physical body. It can be a damning thing, an emotion that holds a dead person in place when all they really want to do is move on."*

Willow swallowed. Anan and Chiwa had gravitated toward each other and moved off to one side, where they seemed to be content to sit and stare and wait patiently until Willow was finished with the problem of Flo. That was good, because right now, all Willow could focus on was the words she'd just heard. It took everything she had to make the next sentence come out of her mouth. "S-so, you want to m-move on."

"Yes."

No hesitation whatsoever, and that, perhaps more

than a lot of other things, really hurt. She shouldn't do it, but subconsciously Willow just had to give it one more try. "You don't . . . you don't want to stay here with me."

"No."

Another critical stab to her heart, and now all Willow wanted to do was roll into a ball and cry like a two-year-old. She and Tara were supposed to have been soul mates, together forever, but hearing the truth—that such feelings and promises didn't carry over to whatever other side awaited after death—was nearly unbearable. For God's sake, all of man- and woman-kind functioned on just that ideal. If it wasn't true, then why bother?

"It isn't that I don't love you," the Ghost of Tara offered, *"but that my love has changed to something more—how can I put it?—Nonmaterial, something that no longer needs the physical manifestations that you crave. What I feel for you now will carry forever, but you cannot understand it until your time comes."*

Willow straightened her shoulders, not feeling a bit comforted by the Ghost of Tara's words. "You're right—I don't understand it. And since that's the way it is, I just have to go by what I know—the here and now—and let eternity take care of itself."

"Give up your idea of resurrecting me and I will be able to leave," the Ghost of Tara said. She sounded small and plaintive. *"Don't you understand, Willow? It is not your love, but your obsession, that traps me here when I need to cross over."*

But Willow had already hardened her heart. "I will

not give you up, Tara. Not now, not tomorrow. Not until I get the rest of your life that should have been mine—*ours*—to share together."

The Ghost of Tara shook her head vehemently. *"Willow—please. You've seen what happens firsthand when you call upon forces to help you that should not be disturbed."* The specter waived a semitransparent hand at Flo, still twisting on the floor, then at Spike. *"Do I need to remind you about Buffy—about how that very nearly backfired on you, and how you pulled her from what should have been her eternal peace because you so wrongly thought she was stranded in a worse dimension when she was better off where she was?"*

"I won't make that same mistake again," Willow said flatly. "I assumed the spell had failed, and I didn't follow through on it. It was a stupid mistake."

"And tell me, Willow, how do you know that I am not better off where I am?"

Willow lifted her chin. "Because, Tara, if you were, you wouldn't be here *now*." With that, Willow strode away from the Ghost of Tara and over to where Flo shuddered. For now, the Ghost of Tara didn't follow.

"Flo," Willow said loudly. "Flo, can you understand me? It's Willow, remember? You're back home now, away from . . ." She hesitated, not sure what to say when she actually had no idea where the woman had been or what she was safe *from*. "From that other place," she finally continued. "And you're safe. Everything is all right now."

But Willow might as well have been talking to a hard-boiled egg. There wasn't a shred of recognition or coherence in Flo's eyes, no hint of civility or even language in the guttural grunts and snapping sounds coming out of her mouth. With a start, Willow realized that most of Flo's teeth were broken, and the skin of her face wasn't just dirty, it was hideously bruised. She leaned closer, trying to see, then recoiled when Flo tried to bite her. Even so, that glance had told her something she didn't want to know, something that really trebled the guilt ratio she was already feeling over losing her coven members.

Flo's tongue had been cut out.

Willow wiped a hand across her own face, feeling perspiration coat her palm even though it was cool in the loft. She needed to do something about Flo, yet there was nothing she could think of that would undo the damage here—scrapes and bruises and minor cuts were one thing, but she had no spell that would immediately reconstitute the severed flesh and restore the woman's mental sensibilities. Such a thing would take time, and a lot of it. Had she been capable of doing so, Willow would have teleported both Flo and herself right into Giles's bedroom at Buffy's, just so Mr. Righteous could see up close and personal the results of what he'd done. Eye for an eye did *not* apply here; Flo hadn't done a thing in the world to hurt him or the rest of Buffy's gang and, had things gone the way Willow had planned—the way they *should* have—she never would have. Her purpose, like all the other Wiccans, was more to feed Willow's abilities than to bother with anyone else.

The Ghost of Tara's whispered words floated past

her ear. *"Let her sleep, Willow. In sleep, she may at least find a temporary peace."*

Willow balled her fists. So much anger—hers, Flo's, no doubt Anan and Chiwa were next on the upcoming anger management agenda. But the Ghost of Tara was right; Willow couldn't fix Flo, but neither would she kill one of her own for no good reason.

She relaxed her hands and lifted them upward, as though she were about to give a blessing to a crowd of people. Below her, Flo's struggles within the blue-light binding doubled, as if the young Wiccan believed she was about to be struck, or worse.

"Shhhhh," Willow told Flo softly. *"Somnus . . . jam diu."* Sleep . . . for a long time.

Chapter Three

Willow thought that in the full light of day that Anan and Chiwa didn't really look so bad. The worst of their wounds had been bandaged and the two women were showered and dressed in clean, new clothes. Things were going to be more or less okay.

Which just goes to show how hope can sometimes taint the logic of a reasonable person.

If she'd thought her other remaining Wiccans were angry with her for allowing Giles and Buffy's little lackeys to get up and do their damage, Willow discovered that their feelings were nothing but mini-irritations compared to these two gals. And it didn't help that in the short time they'd spent together before Giles had sent them off to nightmare land, Anan and Flo had become fast friends. Not lovers—not yet—but they had most definitely been headed in that direction. The discovery of this, even though lacquered with Anan's fury over Flo's current condition, still raised a secret pang of ugly envy in Willow's heart. It had nothing to do with Flo, of course; it was just jealousy that other people might share the type of thing that she and Tara had once experienced but no longer could.

But that would change someday, someday soon, and so Willow would not let that cloud her thinking now.

Willow had healed the visible injuries on all of them, although she hadn't been able to do anything about Chiwa's three broken ribs except tape them up and make her comfortable. Then, of course, there was the matter of Flo's missing tongue. Willow had made a sort of bed out of a long, narrow table against one of the walls in her sleeping area by spreading three thick velvet quilts on it. That was where Flo rested now, her 'sleep' more accurately a possibly permanent state of catatonia. Willow had stayed with the blue theme: deep blue quilts, a long, ocean-colored dress with matching ribbons twined in Flo's now clean and short hair—they'd struggled to remove all the odd things tangled in it and had finally given in and simply cut it. Her skin was also clean and free of marks, although nothing Willow had tried lessened the dark, bruised-looking circles under the comatose young woman's eyes.

At first weeping over Flo's unconscious form, Anan, formerly a quiet little thing with china-pale skin, blond hair, and crystalline blue eyes, had found her land legs, so to speak, and she looked like some sort of mini-Swedish hellion.

"I want revenge," she said. "I want that librarian to

pay for what he did to her—to *us*." At her side, Chiwa nodded, although Willow thought that in reality this one simply seemed happy to be where things were fairly normal again. She was agreeing only because she thought she should. "This cannot go unpunished," Anan continued. "Look at what's happened to her. *He* did that, and he has to pay for it!"

"She will heal eventually," Willow said. "The sleeping spell I cast will also help her flesh reform itself—even her teeth will regenerate. But it will take a long, long time."

"That's not the point!" Anan jerked her chin toward Flo's sleeping form. "She should have justice!"

Sitting across from her, Willow rubbed her forehead and tried to think, to focus. She needed sleep—the spell last night had taken a lot out of her, as had this morning's cleanup of the three Wiccans. It was almost noon, and she didn't think she'd been to bed since the morning before last.

"I say we go over there tonight." Anan sat back and stared hard at Willow. "If I have to, I will go alone."

Willow sighed. "Giles will destroy you, Anan," she said. "He's much more powerful than you." She waved her hand at the loft. It was slowly being refurnished, but there were plenty of empty shelves and spaces where the contents had been sucked away during Giles's spell. "Isn't what he did to you and the others—to Flo—enough evidence? Surely you learned from it."

"Oh, I *learned* all right." Anan's face twisted. "I learned that you care more about yourself and about your ghost than us. And then there's that Slayer—"

Willow held up a hand. "Stop, right now." Her lips were drawn into a tight line across her face. "I've had this conversation already with the other women, and I'm not going to recap it. What's happened has happened, and whining about it isn't going to undo it. What we do now is move on and be very careful to ensure that we don't go through a rerun performance."

Anan looked like she wanted to say more, but Chiwa reached out and put a hand on her arm. "Let it go," she said. "Willow's right. Nothing you do now will change the past."

But Anan's knuckles were white where her hands gripped the edge of the table. "He should *pay*," she insisted. Her gaze found the Ghost of Tara, then turned back to bore into Willow. "Surely you, of all people, can understand that."

"Oh, I do," Willow assured her. "But I also understand that there's nothing I can do about vengeance on the other two men who helped cause Tara's death." *For now,* she said to herself. *For now.* Aloud, she continued, "That means I turn my attention toward something I *can* change, such as resurrecting Tara."

"I can't come back," the Ghost of Tara's voice said in her ear. It was unnerving how one second she could be across the room, then in a blink of an eye, be at Willow's side. Still, Willow supposed that's what ghosts did, and really, she pretty much followed suit with teleporting. Perhaps it was startling only because it was someone else doing it to *her* rather than the other way around.

"Now is not the time to argue about this," she said to the Ghost of Tara in as low a voice as she could.

While on the surface it seemed like the spirit was acquiescing to her wishes, Willow recognized the look the Ghost of Tara gave her as one not of surrender, but of pity. She felt the muscles across the back of her neck tense, but she said nothing; someday, someday soon, the Ghost of Tara would understand that she *would* succeed. Why? Because not succeeding was simply not an option.

"I will restore our coven to its former strength," Willow said loudly, intentionally pulling the conversation back to the coven and away from the Ghost of Tara and matters of earthly revenge and rebirth. She looked at Anan and her expression softened. "I do understand your pain, and we—both of us—will have our time of revenge." Her eyes once again grew steely. "But my goal comes first, above all things, all the time. There will be no exceptions. Revenge will have to wait." She paused, and added, "And for the waiting, perhaps it will be that much sweeter."

Anan didn't respond, but there was no mistaking the gleam of resentment smoldering in her eyes.

"Hello, Amy."

Willow wasn't surprised to see Amy Madison jerk her head around in shock when she heard Willow say her name. "Willow!"

Willow glided through the doorway into Amy's living room without being asked—a nice little benefit about being Wiccan rather than vampire. The front door to Amy's house had been locked, of course, but it might as well have been held in place by a spider web. She would have thought Amy would use an entry protection spell or something of that ilk, but apparently Amy had a lot more confidence in herself than Willow thought she should. Or maybe she just knew it was a lost cause and she hadn't even bothered.

Amy stared at her. "I'd heard rumors," she finally said. "I had no idea they were true."

Willow only smiled more widely. "Oh, I'm sure they are—all of them."

Amy frowned, but Willow was sure she saw her swallow, unintentionally telegraphing how nervous she was. The young woman looked good, as though the home-based magicks practice she'd set up was treating her well. There was no sign of the addiction that they'd both had during what Willow mentally called The Reign of Rack; Amy's auburn hair was clean and nicely styled to frame her face, her makeup was meticulously applied, and her clothes were neat, with an emphasis toward blending in with the crowd rather than being a stand-out Wiccan practitioner. Yeah, Amy was definitely on the road to straight and narrow.

Alas, Willow was here to add a few sharp and exciting curves.

As Willow had come in, Amy had been getting ready to work a spell of some sort, and now Willow wandered over to the table in front of Amy and inspected the contents. Interesting but simple, a little banishment and truth spell that Amy was, perhaps, being paid to work on someone's ex-boyfriend or spouse. A black candle, various ingredients including smelly aseyfatida, nightshade, vinegar, and more, and a small handful of metal implements to be used at various times during the rendering of her enchantment. In the overall scheme of things, it probably seemed truly big-time to whomever was channeling a few bucks toward Amy, but in reality? Extremely small potatoes.

"Nice work," Willow said, but she didn't really mean it. Her next words drove that home. "But why are you wasting your time with stuff like this when you could come out and play with the big guys?"

"Meaning . . . you?" Amy said carefully.

Willow gave her a little sideways smile, but she didn't answer. Instead she picked up the small, dark wood statue that was amid the items arranged on the tabletop. It seemed to be the center of attention, so she examined it closely. "Is this him?" she asked. "The object of your little spell?" She put just the tiniest of extra emphasis on the word *little*.

Reluctantly, Amy nodded. "Yes. But you don't have to—"

Willow dismissed Amy's words with a flick of her hand, then folded her fingers around the warm wooden figurine. She squeezed and a second later the color of the wood changed to a deep, fiery glow.

"Wait," said Amy. "He isn't that—"

There was a dark puff of smoke above Willow's hand and she opened her fingers. A blackened chunk of something that resembled coal fell and bounced across the surface of the table.

"Bad," Amy finished morosely.

"Oops," Willow said. There was absolutely no emotion in her voice.

Amy shook her head in disgust and swept everything on the table aside; it was certainly of no use to her now. "Hell's bells," she muttered. "Now what am I supposed to tell his girlfriend, huh? She only wanted to keep him from going into the Bronze without her. What'd you do to him, anyway? Send him to Timbuktu?"

Willow raised an eyebrow. So Amy *did* know the real lowdown on the recent events at the home loft. "Not my problem," she said. "And it shouldn't be yours, either. It's time for you to leave this amateur stuff behind."

Amy sat back and folded her arms. "And what? Become one of your little Wiccan slaves? I suppose that's what you came here for, isn't it? To force me to join the pack?"

Willow shrugged. "I'd rather it was voluntary."

Amy laughed humorlessly. "Oh, really. The whole Wiccan community has heard about your methods of persuasion, Willow. Worse than that are the rumors that while he didn't break up the whole thing, Giles still nearly managed to destroy it all. Everyone says it's like he bounces—you can put him in a wheelchair, but you can't bring him down all the way."

Willow chuckled, but like Amy, she wasn't finding any of this particularly amusing. "How and when I deal with Rupert Giles is my business," she said shortly. She was struggling mightily not to show how much it bothered her to have his victories thrown in her face by someone else. "He's a meddlesome old man who'll eventually get his due. Right now I have other things upon which I want to concentrate." She paused. "And that's where you come in."

Amy looked at her slyly. "I'm going to help you 'concentrate.'"

It wasn't a question, and they both knew it. "Exactly."

But Amy had yet to be persuaded. "So what's in it for me?" She held up a finger before Willow could answer. "Please. I've heard all the talk about the threats and bubbling skin and all that. Yeah, you could make me into today's tapioca pudding pile, but then what good would I be?" She shrugged. "We both know that the first person you force into labor is the last person you can trust."

Willow nodded. "Very true," she agreed. She stared into space, as though she were trying to concentrate. "Hmmmm. What *would* be in it for you, Amy? For that matter, for any of you?" She pulled a forefinger idly along the edge of Amy's table and a small line of fire followed it. Out of the corner of her eye, she saw the other Wiccan cautiously backing away. Abruptly Willow snapped her fingers and the pattern of miniflames disappeared. "What do you want? Fame? Fortune? Love?" Willow shrugged. "I'm not promising any of that." She glanced at Amy, and for a brief second, a shadow of the disappeared flames danced in her eyes. "The point *is*, Amy, you were my friend. If I come to you for help with something as important as raising Tara from the dead, an event that is so momentous to me that it has overtaken everything else in my life, that should be enough. Yeah, I could threaten . . . but do I really have to? I don't think so. I shouldn't need to threaten, or beg, or use trickery. The old friendship should be enough."

When Amy only looked at her, a corner of Willow's mouth turned up. "I should have known the friendship angle wasn't going to fly. It always did singe your edges that I was more powerful than you. You must really be burning now, with the way things turned out." Willow paused for a few seconds, studying the carpet around her thoughtfully. "All right," she said. "Then look at it this way. Outside of me, you're probably the second most powerful Wiccan in Sunnydale. Yes, I can do this without you. Eventually, I could probably do it alone, if I really had to. It will just happen so much faster with a little help, not just from others, but from powerful Wiccans." When Amy was still silent, Willow let her gaze drop to her hands. "You realize, of course, that once this is done, I'm likely to be out of the Wiccan scene forever. I mean, Tara wanted me to quit the magick altogether, and I think it's a pretty good bet she hasn't changed her tune to angel and organ music just because she's dead." She paused to let that sink in. "When Tara is back, you're it, Amy. It all falls to you."

While Amy made a show of glancing around her small living room regretfully, Willow definitely had put a gleam in the other woman's eye. Finally, Amy inhaled. "All right. But . . . *one month*. That's all, Willow." The look she gave Willow was half warning, half resentment. "I'm not signing on to be your indentured servant for the next damned decade. If you still can't figure it out by then, even with all the power you're pulling together, I'm out of here. And by all rights, you should let the others go, too."

Willow started to open her mouth to say *No way*, but then she stopped. What was the point of arguing? Let Amy think she was agreeing, but the woman was a fool if she thought she—or any of the others—was going anywhere until Willow was damned well ready to let them go. She could easily crush the others into submission, and even banded together they would not be able to overtake her. Whether or not she wanted to keep surrounding herself with a bunch of women who hated her was another question; as if figuring out the spell wasn't difficult enough, that kind of negative energy directed toward her could easily get out of control. If it really came down to it, she might well release them all and start over, but it would be her decision, not Amy's.

"All right," Willow said. "One month. Get your things together. You've got a deal."

Two more members, and her coven would once again be at full strength. She already had two women in mind for the last empty slots, medium-strength Wiccans that Njeri had mentioned because, as Willow had pointed out to Amy, Njeri also wanted this to be over with so she could get on with her life. In that was the perfect example of trust betrayed—while on the surface Njeri claimed to be friends with the two she'd told Willow about, she was still essentially "giving them up" so she could move her own freedom more quickly toward the realm of reality.

Willow was finally ready to return to the problem of collecting the massive amount of power needed to resurrect Tara. In the meantime, there was one little problem that she needed to take care of, to ensure there wasn't a repeat of the other night.

Giles.

Chapter Four

This was something Willow really wanted to do alone. She ached to send them all away, to have silence and no one—save the ever-present Ghost of Tara—watching over her, scrutinizing her methods, learning her secrets, secretly criticizing, and offering suggestions. But as it seemed to be with many of the other oh-so-important issues in her life, apparently it was not to be. She could insist—she could do anything she wanted—but after all, Willow had promised them her protection. Did they not deserve to be present during the creation of the living instrument that would perform exactly that function?

Still, she ensured that she was mostly undisturbed.

"There will be no talking," she told the other women of the coven. "No comments on the spell or my choice of words, no suggestions from anyone. There shall be no whispering among yourselves, or even so much as a cough to break my concentration. The nature of the creature that I am creating is intensely personal, and it cannot be shared. It can be created by only one person, and it will obey only its creator." She gave them all a hard look. "Me."

No one said anything, but there were a number of uneasy looks exchanged as they positioned themselves just outside Willow's smoothly drawn circle of scarlet sand. They were remembering, of course, the difficulty Willow had experienced in dealing with the birth of the *sine kot diabl*, the brilliant blue cat-creature they had helped Willow create and that had, at the end, not only disobeyed her, but turned and attacked her. Willow couldn't blame them for the recollection, but hopefully their main focus on the memory would be Buffy's presence and the damage done to them by Giles's nearly devastating spell. Willow didn't want to focus on her own past failures or disappointment right now, didn't want the negative energy and bad memories of such things to pollute the life force she was going to channel into the inanimate materials carefully set out in front of her.

She had prepared herself meticulously, bathing in water purified by sea salt and donning an earth tone robe that she'd never before worn. Made of deep gold velvet trimmed in heavy satin, it draped on the floor at her feet like the last rays of an autumn sunset. Everything about her exuded warmth, from the thick material to the body heat building beneath the outfit; this was good, because heat was one of the wonderful basic things that sustained life—witness the coldness of the vampire's bloody kiss and embrace. In addition to that, Willow wanted to *bond* with this creature, to infuse it with every bit of herself that she could possibly think of. That way, she reasoned, there would be no chance of a rebellion, like the one with which her *sine kot diabl* had so surprised her. This was also the reason she would allow none of the other Wiccans to help in calling forth the spirit she would force to animate it. This one would be hers and hers alone.

Willow had lined the wooden floor with a large, white plastic tarp. In the center of the tarp, culled in equal amounts from seven of the twelve graveyards in Sunnydale by a series of spells she'd performed very early this morning, was a dark mound of moist earth. Graveyards were a common thing in Sunnydale—the vamps made sure of that. Still, what she'd gathered had represented only seventy percent of the home earth she'd needed. Willow had pulled the remainder from somewhere far more special, a venue near and dear to many in the now splintered Scooby Gang.

Some time back, there had been a group of military-oriented monster hunters in Sunnydale. Perhaps "monster hunters" wasn't precisely the correct term, but it covered a lot of what they'd believed was their mission and what they'd done. Called the Initiative, the group had performed experiments on demons of all kinds, even putting a control chip in her little Spikey Pet's head to force him to be a vampire good guy.

But the Initiative's dream had ultimately been

decreed a failure by one of the higher secret muckity-mucks, and for good reason: Its mainstay had been a creature that was part demon, part human, and part robot; named Adam, the thing had gotten completely out of control, using its intelligence to scheme and its strength and size to kill anyone within its reach, including one of the professors at the college who had been secretly involved in the whole thing. Finally destroyed by Buffy at the end of a huge battle that had left nearly half of the Initiative's soldiers dead, the result had been *hasta la Initiative*. There had been talk of filling the secret underground compound with concrete, but Willow had been too smart to believe that costly cover-up had ever been done. Her hunch had proved correct; still underground, the formerly glorious compound that had been filled with computers and priceless medical equipment was now in ruins, everything inside devastated by the soldiers' final battle with the demons Adam had set free.

But the floor was still earthen, and it was still saturated with blood and memories—specific memories, for which Willow had a very strong use. Smiling with satisfaction, she'd drawn the last thirty percent of what she'd needed from the floor where the final, gruesome battle had taken place.

The mass had been sifted clean of roots, worms, insects, and pebbles, even bone fragments, but there was no spell that could remove the history from within the earth, the actual physical evidence of the men who had fought and died in that spot. The soil was soaked with dried blood, power, and residual spirits, and it was exactly what Willow needed.

Tonight, Willow would make her very own golem.

According to history, there were a lot of different ways to create a golem, most stemming from the simple forming of a crude figure that was mostly brawn and not much brains, and which then ran amok on its creator's command and terrorized everything in its path. Some even claimed that Mary Shelley's mythical Frankenstein was actually a form of golem, and by that token, Willow supposed that Adam could have the golem-son of the now defunct Initiative. Born of Mother Earth's elemental magick, golems were generally extremely difficult or impossible to destroy, and oftentimes the architect behind the golem held the only key to stopping it. In that part, Willow was well pleased—she wanted no one to be able to put down her newest little pet but her. But as to the other aspects . . . no way would she allow some conglomeration of mud and spirit to go lumbering around Sunnydale without some semblance of purpose—her purpose.

Magick, especially the darker form of it, was a wonderful thing. While a lot of it was hammered in the stones of the ages, there were other parts—great chunks—that could be molded and shaped and changed to suit the practitioner's particular desire. Willow's golem would not be a dull-witted creature let loose with its only perceived purpose to crush and smash and destroy. Oh no—her creation would be well formed; it would have intelligence and logic and a familiar, courageous spirit, one with whom Willow had once walked side by side in this world. It was that familiarity, that recognition, that Willow was certain would allow her to control it.

Working slowly and carefully, Willow picked up the first of her pitchers of undiluted and blessed seawater and poured it over the mini-mountain of earth. Wisely, the other Wiccans stayed quiet, not even daring to talk among themselves, too afraid to break her concentration. She began to knead the mound of dirt, adding more seawater a little at a time. She had to be careful to get the ratio just right. If it was too runny, her golem wouldn't be able to hold its form; it would be like the melting man, leaving a nasty, muddy trail everywhere it went. Too dry and pieces of it would crack away, especially if it had to engage someone in battle. The creature's birthing form had to be smooth and pliable, the consistency of firm bread dough.

Stretching and patting and rounding, Willow put everything she had into this project. She was good with her hands, but she'd never had to be *this* good—sculpting talents weren't high on her list. Sometime in second or third grade she'd tried to make a doll out of Play-Doh, working diligently along with the rest of her classmates to complete her personal little project. It had been a disaster—she'd had no idea that mixing green and red would give her gray (although that color had been very close to what she was working on now), and instead of the little red-haired clay doll with the green hat she'd been aiming for, Willow had ended up with a gray-skinned mass that looked a lot like your common variety of garden rock. Later she'd tried again, this time with bread dough and a sort of preteen voodoo cookie doll in mind. Alas, her sculpting skills hadn't improved any, and God knows where she'd gotten the idea at twelve that she could actually bake.

Now, however, she would not be so lost, and she really didn't care what color the golem's skin turned out to be.

The head started to take shape and Willow didn't stop to worry about features—she would come back to that in a bit. Broad shoulders and a nicely muscled chest and arms, sturdy forearms—he would need all that to give him strength. She was finding it much easier to work life size, really getting into it. A small-ish waist just because that was an unspoken require-ment on any hunky man-model, and good, firm hips and legs to give him strength and balance. Once com-pleted, she returned to the golem's face. Let's be honest—she really didn't want to have to look at some misshapen, ugly monster mug every morning, noon, and night for the next . . . well, however long he was useful.

As she worked on this final aspect of the golem, Willow began to hum an enchantment spell beneath her breath, sing-songing the words over and over while she focused. She'd decreed that the other Wiccans had to stay on the far outside of the circle, and that was a good thing—no matter how sharp their hearing, they would never pick up the mumbled, intentionally slurred syllables.

"Formed of ashes and dust, your true body now gone, heed my call and return, to be mine as reborn.

Formed of ashes and dust, your true body now gone, heed my call and return, to be mine as reborn. Formed of . . ."

It didn't take long for the murmured words to become automatic. Over and over, she chanted while her thoughts couldn't help but skitter along the rough edges of reality.

Riley Finn.

Former star soldier of the Initiative, one of only a very few men to have been close enough with Buffy to share her bed. Being a superpowerful Wiccan had its perks, and little did Miss Smartie Slayer know that Willow had access to a few levels of the metaphysical that imparted the all-knowing with some info about which Buffy had no idea, like the fact that the last time Buffy had seen Riley and his wife, Sam, as they left for Nepal on their upcoming demon hunt, was the last time she would ever see them alive. Both had been toasted—literally—by a Nepalese flarewing, a fire-spewing demon against whom the two had never stood a chance. Raised from the depths of hell by a local warlord to aid him in his quest for power, the creature, which flew with the speed of a hummingbird but was half the size of a man, was ultimately destroyed by Riley's unit, but that moment of victory came about fifteen minutes too late for the happy Finn couple. Too bad, so sad.

Willow wasn't much interested in what had waited for Sam on the other side of the veil of death. But she was very, *very* interested in Riley Finn. For Riley, she had a little side trip planned.

Her golem was nearly finished, and if she had to say so herself, she'd done a pretty passable job of constructing Riley Finn's features out of the mud-mixture of seawater and Sunnydale soil. She wasn't Michelangelo, but she wasn't the grade-school bookworm anymore, either. She kept the proportions correct and her hands made the right dips and curves, although they wouldn't quite follow what her mind's eye wanted to see in terms of exact resemblance. There might have been a few lumps and bulges here and there that didn't want to come out, but once she finished with the spell that would place Riley's spirit into the mud-man, Willow had an idea that his specter would blur a lot of that away and he'd become recognizable.

There were a number of reasons she'd chosen Riley. First and foremost, he was dead. Yes, in life he had been more attuned to Buffy, but he had also known Willow, and fairly well. That should give her a good connection, something that would go beyond what she considered the rather mundane power of the binding spell. As a member of the Initiative, one of Riley's major duties had been to protect the unsuspecting— and sometimes the suspecting—against demons and evil in general. While Willow and her coven members might or might not be considered innocents, depending on who you were talking to, they still needed protection. As a protector golem, Riley would be galvanized into action by the fear of those to whom he was bound and by the orders of his creator.

And, of course, there was the matter of pleasing the Ghost of Tara. Always in the back of her mind, this wasn't something that Willow decided to share with the others, but it was a big factor in her choice. As the coven's protector, Riley would do battle with anything and anyone to protect them, even Buffy. Yet as Buffy's former lover, it seemed a fair bet that while he'd fight the Slayer and pummel her a good one, he probably wouldn't kill her or any of the other people he'd once known in his earthly life; after the debacle with the *sine kot diabl*, Willow wasn't seeking a down and dirty evil here. In short, he would do the job for which Willow was creating him: keep the Slayer and her minions away, and keep her coven members Giles-free.

There, she thought as she patted the last of the wet earth into place. *An empty vessel, all ready and waiting to be filled.*

Lifeless and earthen brown, the golem lay there, completely devoid of motion. At her right hand was a sterling silver ceremonial knife with a pearl handle above the long, clean blade. Moving deliberately, Willow lifted it and slowly made a deep, six-inch incision down the center of the golem's life-size chest, right where there would have been a breastbone in a real man. Nothing happened, of course—the Riley golem was still nothing but dirt and water and wishes. But that would change very shortly.

She set the blade aside and used her fingers to work the incision apart until it looked like a dark, nasty wound. When it was opened enough, she made a small mixture from several waiting bowls of secret Ashkenazi herbs and salts. Once that was completed, she filled the lesion with her compound, being very, very careful not to spill any of it outside of the chest area. That done, Willow moistened her fingers with seawater then dipped them into another waiting bowl, this one filled with unadulterated sea salt—a cure for the wound. She pressed the edges of the hole together and worked at them carefully until only a barely noticeable mound remained. Like a scar, or even a grave, once something—no matter how small—was set inside it, that space would never again appear normal.

There were only a few more steps to go. Inside a tiny, lacquered wooden box was a piece of parchment, folded in half, and older than old. Willow slid the top off and lifted the paper free, barely touching it with the tips of her fingernails; even so, she could feel the fragile sliver of paper wanting to crack at her touch. Of the things she was including in tonight's enchantment, this was by far the most valuable, nearly priceless. Written inside the folded area, or so she was told, was the secret name of God according to a long extinct sect of European Jews from the Middle Ages. She had no definite proof of this, but the parchment had come from a reliable and rather pricey source, whose own vast demonic power made them a little on the indifferent side to what Willow had to offer. Still, they were not impervious to her anger, so she tended to believe the document was what it was. To read the name would render it commonly known and therefore useless, so that wasn't even a consideration.

Operating at the speed of a snail, Willow gingerly tucked the piece of paper into the shallow opening she had fashioned for the Riley golem's mouth, letting it pull moisture from its surroundings and her seawater-wet fingers until it was pliable enough to press and mold against the inside surface of the cheek she was forming along the way. That done, she picked up the ceremonial knife again, this time wielding it like a sharp-tipped ink pen. With more care than she had ever done anything before—or at least it seemed that way—she fashioned three letters into the surface across the golem's forehead:

תמא

Willow set the knife aside and stepped back, speaking the carved words under her breath. It was so faint that she may have been the only one who noticed it, but as the last sound passed her lips, she saw the faintest of glows settled around her sculpture's coarse facial features, then disappear. After a moment's pause, she leaned over the Riley golem's mouth and spoke, letting her life-breath flow into its mouth along with her words, knowing her dark energy would caress the ancient paper lining the inside of its newly made cheek. "Come to me, Riley Finn," she whispered. "Leave your sleep behind until you are permitted to return, for you have been called and bound to me, compelled to obey my will as I see fit. *You* will *come to me now!*"

Willow felt the golem's response before she saw it. It was without a doubt one of the strangest things she'd ever experienced, a sort of fine-tuned vibration in her body that went all the way down to her bones, yet wasn't present in the floor on which she stood. She could tell that the others in the room felt it too—their surprised expressions and the miniature muscle jerks gave it away in an instant.

But all of that was secondary compared to their reaction when Willow's Riley-golem opened a pair of suddenly very alive, clear hazel eyes and sat up.

Chapter Five

"This," Giles said, holding up a small, gleaming, dark red bottle of something, "is what's going to make the spell work this time."

Anya, ever curious, leaned forward across the table and held out her hand. Giles obligingly set the bottle on her palm and she peered at it. Not much to see—there was no label and it was the glass that was colored, masking the contents. She couldn't view inside the bottle, although there was a faint vaguely familiar smell—a little bloody, but not quite. She knew better than to open the bottle without being told it was all right. "Okay, I'll bite," she finally said. "What is it? Some kind of poison? Because while I like to win as much as the next girl, I'm really all against the whole permanent death thing. We've kind of had enough of that around here."

"Of course it's not poison." Giles shot her a reproachful look. "It's dragon's blood. And a particularly fine specimen of it, I might add."

Next to Anya, Xander rolled his eyes. "Okay, now I think I've finally heard everything. Dragons? What are we into here? *Dragonlance*? *Dungeons and Dragons*? Or are we making up our own?" He raked both hands impatiently through his hair. "Next we'll be talking about—"

"Vampires? Demons?"

He stared at Buffy, then glanced at Anya for support. No help there—her expression was totally *You're on your own*.

"Precisely," Giles said in a voice that was just a little too hearty. "Six or seven years ago you would have thought a person insane had they informed you that vampires and demons really existed. Now you take that fact for granted every day, because you've seen these beasts for yourself." Giles took off his glasses and pulled a handkerchief from his pocket so he could polish the lenses energetically. "Surely in that short time you haven't become convinced that just because you can't see something, it doesn't exist."

Dawn raised an eyebrow. "Can you say free ticket on the express train to harm?"

Xander started to retort, then decided not to. First of all, those six or seven years hadn't exactly flown by—that period of time seemed way long to him. Secondly, just because *he* didn't believe meant it was a job requirement for the others. Still, the idea of something like a dragon, maybe something fire-breathing and huge like out of that movie, *Reign of Fire*? Great special effects, but not, as Giles would say, bloody likely. One or two demons à la Mayor Wilkins—which, since Wilkins had turned into a giant snake with the intention of eating the town, was hardly your garden variety— maybe. But this? *Flying dragon?* Nah. Still, since it would have been useless to argue, he let a shoulder shrug close out the matter on his end.

"So," Buffy said, sitting forward and eyeing the bottle, "what does this something add to the nothing that was there before?"

"Excellent question," Giles noted as he shoved his glasses back into place on the bridge of his nose. "Speed, for one. Strength, for another. And then speed, speed, and more speed."

Anya brightened. "Of course! Had we been able to open the portal quicker the first time, most—maybe all—of Willow's coven would have been sucked into forever-never land before she ever got the chance to come back upstairs."

Giles started to say something in response, but Dawn's soft words cut him off. "I have a question." When they all looked at her expectantly, she let her gaze drop to the floor, as if what she were about to say was somehow difficult. "Where did they *go*?"

Xander, Buffy, and Anya only looked at her blankly, but Giles frowned uncomfortably. "Go?"

Dawn nodded. "Yeah. Go. As in end of journey, destination Shangri-la, or whatever. Where did you send them?"

"Well, I . . ." The librarian's voice faded and he blinked as he realized he couldn't answer.

"Wow," Anya said in a surprised voice. "You don't even know?"

Xander looked from Giles to Anya. "Okay, so call me the guy who's not always high on the magick meter, but isn't that kind of a dangerous thing?"

Even Buffy scowled. "Are we talking alternate dimensions here? Past? Future? Hell?"

Anya tossed her head. "Why ask him? He's already admitted he hasn't a clue." She waved a hand in the air. "They could've popped into being right over the mouth of a Sloggoth demon." At their questioning looks, she explained, "They have lots of teeth. And look like giant worms. The girls probably made a very tasty meal."

Giles's expression was shocked. "They did not!" He flushed. "What I mean to say is that I would never send them to another dimension without being absolutely sure where they were going. It's far too dangerous." He rubbed at the bridge of his nose as if he had a headache. "I admit I didn't have time to precisely direct them, but I did manage to keep them here on Earth. I felt they'd at least have a better chance of being safe."

Buffy's frown deepened. "I may not make the dean's list in geography, but even I know there's some pretty scary places on the globe. Yeah, they'd kind of fallen in with the crappy side of Willow, but I thought we'd figured out it wasn't their choice. I mean, if you didn't have all this premapped out, they could've ended up anywhere—"

"And we did."

Anya gasped as Giles, in a move showing admirable dexterity, jerked his chair away from the table and spun it to face their unexpected visitor. Buffy stood as well, automatically going into a defensive stance, while Xander and Dawn just sat and stared.

The young woman facing them was quite beautiful, if you were the type who went for that slightly gaunt, haunted look. Xander thought she even looked a little on the elfin side, like an escapee from *Lord of the Rings*. She was thin and pale, with hair so light it was nearly white. If tropical ocean water could be solidified and polished, it would probably match the color of the blue eyes that stared back at them, although the word "tropical" gave the idea of warmth where that wasn't present in this woman's gaze. Beneath that lovely ocean-water gaze were shadows that told of times much harder than any of them could guess.

"You see," the young woman said after giving them a few seconds to study her, "I'm one of those women in Willow's coven." She fastened her gaze on Giles. "You know, the ones you sent off into the ether without having the decency to *think* about what you were doing?" She paced in front of the group but didn't try to get any closer. Ten steps one way, turn, ten steps back, turn, then start all over. Each time she turned, the black cape and long, forest green dress she was wearing billowed behind her, her feathery hair a sharp contrast against the dark fabric.

"So I thought I'd drop in for a visit and tell you all about it," she continued. "What it was like, what I saw.

The people who greeted me—especially that—and how long I was there." Her eyes met each of theirs.

Giles's mouth dropped open. "I don't understand. You say you were, uh, removed by our spell, and yet here you are, obviously unharmed. What's your name? And how did you—"

"Obviously?" The blond witch's eyes darkened to the color of wild storm clouds. *"Nothing* is obvious, Mr. Librarian—not where I was, how I got back, or what the rest of the consequences were." She tossed her head. "But I'm here to change all that."

"Your name—," Giles began.

The young woman shook her head. "Forget it. I know what you're trying to do. Even the youngest witch knows that having knowledge of her name gives one power over her. That's a child's ploy and I won't play that game with you." She gave them all a dark smile. "But I *will* fill you in on the rest of the story. In fact, I can't wait."

Buffy watched her mistrustfully, but Giles was determined to be civil. Perhaps Dawn's words were working on him, firing up that pesky guilty conscience. "Tea," he suggested. "Perhaps you'd like a cup of tea." Always Mr. Manners.

One side of the witch's mouth curled up, and without being invited, she strode past Buffy, pulled out one of the chairs around the table, and settled herself onto it. "I'll pass," she said. Her eyes glittered unpleasantly, betraying a hint of something—insanity? Fury? It was hard to tell the difference. "But please," she said. "Giles, isn't it? You go ahead and enjoy yourself."

Now it was Anya who had run out of patience. "So tell us, already," she said.

"So there I was," said the blond woman, "knee deep in minding my own business. I'm doing my thing, and I'm doing Willow's thing—"

"Which would be what?" Giles asked.

She ignored his question. "When out of the blue, these three"—she swept a hand toward Xander, Anya, and Dawn, apparently not noticing when they flinched; with a Wiccan, a person could never be sure when a hand wave was just a hand wave—"show up and start making a mess of the place and mouthing some kind of relocation ditty. Suddenly, *bam!* I go from being seated in a nice, comfortable chair to being face down in the dirt. It's hot, wet, and tropical, but not in any good kind of way, you know? Bad enough I'm spitting out ants and beetles, but then—oh, wait, did I mention the leeches that dropped out of the trees and landed all over my arms and legs?" She held up one arm and let her loose sleeve fall backward. At random intervals across her porcelain skin were small, puckered pink scars. "And of course there were the poisonous snakes. But they were nothing compared to the natives, who found it really interesting to have this foreign American blond woman basically drop out of the freaking *sky* and into their laps."

"Oh, dear," Giles said in a low voice. "Might I guess . . . Burma, perhaps? Or somewhere in Malaysia?"

The blond-haired witch's eyes blazed. "You're asking *me*? You barge into my life without invitation and send me halfway across the damned globe, and you're asking *me* where I went?"

"Excuse me," Buffy said. "Reality check, okay? Call me paranoid, but somehow I can't believe you dropped in just to tell us about your *Gulliver's Travels*."

"Sounds more like *Lord of the Flies* to me," Dawn said.

Buffy decided to try diplomacy. "Look," she said. "Everything worked out okay. I mean, you're here now, right? You—"

The Wiccan spun to face the Slayer with enough force to startle Buffy, making her automatically step back. "Everything's all *right*? Your librarian pal decides to play supernatural travel agent, and as a result I end up scarred and my girlfriend ends up insane and in a coma, and you say everything's *all right*?" The last of her words was practically a scream.

For a long moment, as her words sank in, no one did anything but stare at her. Then Giles said in a low voice, "I'm so sorry."

But the young woman only laughed shrilly. "You know what? That's just not *good* enough."

There was no warning about the energy ball she flung at him, and it was only Buffy's instinct that saved the former Watcher. That inkling of what might happen, or maybe the tickle at the back of her neck—whatever it was, the indescribable feeling was what made Buffy step smoothly into a sidekick that sent the angry girl tumbling across the room. The zap she'd intended for Giles missed him by a good two feet, although it made Dawn yelp when it came a little too close to her.

"Oh, no, we've been through this before. Uh-uh,

not going to ruin my shop again—" Before the nameless Wiccan could regain her feet and try it again, Anya slid into vengeance demon mode, strode forward, and backhanded her. She raised her hand to do it again, then froze as the air only a few inches away began to sparkle at the same time Giles yelled "Stop!"

Anya backed away but held on to her demon form. "I don't know why you always feel sorry for the underdog," she snapped. "It's obvious she would've killed you." She opened her mouth to say more but surprise choked off her words as Willow's dark-clad figure suddenly formed in front of her.

"Yes, she would have," Willow said. She frowned, but the expression was directed toward the woman on the floor, who was now struggling to sit up. "And been quite happy about it, I'm sure." She made a *tsk* noise as she reached down and yanked her comrade upright with barely any effort at all. "You've been a bad girl, Anan," she admonished. "I specifically told you no payback. At least not right now."

The other woman, Anan, seemed like she wanted to say something but didn't dare. Instead she lowered her eyes and stared resentfully at the floor.

"Hey, wait a minute," Anya protested. "You're telling her it's okay later on?"

Anya flinched when Willow turned her black gaze toward her and shrugged. Her eyes were like flat black stones floating atop the vein-lined skin of her face. She never loosened her vise-grip on Anan's wrist. "What she does after I'm through with her is her business, and eventually that time will come. Until then, she's mine."

She squeezed Anan's wrist for emphasis and the other woman gasped with pain. Willow sent Giles a black-lipped smile before turning it on Anan. "I'm sure she understands that now." She glanced down. "Don't you?"

Another squeeze, and this time Anan barely suppressed an outcry. "Yes!" she blurted. "Yes—I understand!"

"Good," Willow said with satisfaction. "That's a nice, obedient little Wiccan." Her gaze touched each of them, but it was absolutely devoid of any interest until it stopped at Giles. She tilted her head, as if she were considering her words before she spoke. "Don't test me again, Giles," she finally said. "I've no time for your petty war games. My coven is at full number once more. I really suggest you stay away from it."

"Willow—"

"We'll be going now."

"Wait," Giles said. He *had* to know more, to get her to talk. He leaned forward but couldn't get the chair to respond fast enough, couldn't get any closer to Willow. Frustration ate at him. "You said after you're through with her. What exactly are you planning to do—"

But Willow had already shimmered away, and somehow taken Anan with her.

"Well, that was enlightening," Dawn said. She shoved her hands in the pockets of her jeans. "Not."

"We need more information," Giles said. Annoyance was leaking out of his voice. "Much more information."

"Been there, done that," Anya said. "Got the tooth-bite necklace, not doing it again." Then, more to herself, she mumbled, "I can't believe she's powerful enough to teleport someone *with* her. Wow."

"Whatever Willow's doing can't be good," Xander said. "Did you see how cold she was? Like she has no heart."

"I think she has a heart," Dawn said. "I just think it's been hammered so hard that the usual patch-and-glue isn't working."

"I may be way off course here," Giles said suddenly, "but didn't it sound a lot like those women were being held against their will?"

"A Wiccan labor camp," Buffy said. "Yeah, I could see that. Willow's definitely got the power-pack to make it happen."

"But why?" Xander demanded. "You said it: If you want voltage, Willow's already got it. Why does she need the others?"

"To do something hellish," Anya said. She morphed back to human form, then picked up the chair that Anan had overturned in her tumble. "Something she can't do alone because, as much oomph as she has, it just isn't quite on the money to do whatever it is she's got in mind." Anya glanced sideways at Buffy and Giles. "But it won't be long. If she's siphoning off all those Wiccans to add to what she took out of Giles, she's headed toward nuclear. We're talking glow in the dark in no time."

"Then she has to be stopped," Dawn said. She looked from her sister to Giles. "We can't let her get together that much power. Can we?"

Xander's mouth twisted. "I thought you were the Willow champion. All gung-ho on her over-use of the 'punish early, punish often' theory of retribution."

Dawn tossed her head. "Willow's appetite for revenge seems to be rubbing off on her honeybee workers, who're turning into killer bees and trying to sting us."

Giles pulled off his glasses and scrubbed his face hard with his hands, leaving a splotch of red, irritated skin on both cheeks. "Comatose," he muttered, more to himself than the others. He looked up and raised his voice. "Willow's right, you know. I should have had a better idea of where the Wiccans were getting banished to before I armed you guys with that spell."

"What's the difference?" Dawn said. "If they were evil, they deserved whatever they got."

Xander frowned at her. "You sure turned hard case all of a sudden."

Buffy stopped any response Dawn might have had. "That's just it, Dawn—we never knew for sure that they *were* evil. We assumed it. Because Giles didn't . . . uh . . ." She stumbled before she found more diplomatic words. "He didn't realize," she finally managed, "what was going to happen to those women. Well, except for Anan and her friend."

"They could even be dead." Giles's voice was nearly a whisper, but they all heard him.

"Oh, hey," Xander said, but there was a nervousness in his voice that betrayed him. "I'm sure that didn't happen."

"I wouldn't doubt it," Anya said bluntly. "If one of

them came back nutzoid, that's a pretty hard indicator that she didn't spend the time at Disneyland. We sent away five. I don't suppose we know how many Willow managed to bring back?"

Buffy sent Giles a puzzled look. "Yeah, Giles. What's up with that? You didn't say anything about her being able to bring them back once we catapulted them into the land of elsewhere."

Giles took a deep breath. "She wasn't supposed to be able to do so," he admitted. "The spell I used was extremely rare, and a locator spell to counter it is almost unheard of."

"There's that 'almost' word again," Xander said. "Haven't you ever heard that horseshoes and hand grenades thing?"

"Too often." Anya tossed her hair. "You're lucky. She could have made another one of those cat creatures. If you ask me, she took it pretty good."

"Only because she's busy with something else," Buffy pointed out. "Something too big for her to be bothered."

"Always a dangerous thing when we have no idea what that is," Xander agreed.

Giles frowned momentarily, then decided to let Xander's statement pass. "If we can't actually find out what it is, then we'll have to go back in there," Giles said with finality. "We don't have a choice. But after what we've found out, I'm going to modify the spell, put more . . . *specifics* in it. I won't take the chance of harming one of those women again. I'll keep the basics of the spell—dissolution of the coven—the same, but make sure no one's harmed this time. Send them someplace completely nondangerous and benign."

Anya sneered at him. "Somehow I don't think it's going to make much difference on their end. You're forgetting that they were pretty hell-bent on beating the crap out of us."

"Well," Dawn said, "we did barge in there without an invitation."

"And then Anya started in on the chanting," Xander added. "Never a big thing on the house-warming gift list."

"Why is everyone ganging up on *me?*" Anya demanded. She folded her arms and glared at all of them. "Fine. Go ahead and get your asses kicked again, but don't say I didn't warn you."

"We're not going to do it the same way," Giles insisted. "This time it'll be different. We'll—"

"Oh, I heard you the first time," Anya interrupted. "Different. Right." She turned away and stomped off toward the back of the Magic Box. "I'll bring the bandages."

Chapter Six

"**Y**ou had no right to stop me from getting my revenge!" Back at the loft and far from being cowed, Anan was standing tall and strong in front of Willow and the rest of the coven. "You don't *own* me." She jerked a hand toward the other women. "You don't own *any* of us."

Willow folded her hands and regarded the blond witch calmly. "No, of course I don't. But I *do* control you."

Anan shook her head. "Oh no you don't. You just think you do." She lifted her chin. "We could all walk out of here right now, you know. And then where would you be?" She stared at each of her fellow Wiccans in turn, but each woman only lowered her eyes. "Cowards, all of you," she hissed. "She singes a little skin and finds the yellow streak down every one of your backs. She couldn't do a thing to stop us if we all left at once."

But Willow only smiled. "I couldn't? It seems you've forgotten who brought you here to begin with, and that not a one of you came of your own free will, except Amy." She shrugged, and there was something about the move that made the more rebellious of those in the room shift uneasily and glance at one another. "But hey, you want to cruise on out of here, by all means, have at it. In fact, maybe I'll even help you choose your fun-in-the-sun spot. Or maybe just send you back to where one of you has already visited."

Willow closed her eyes briefly, then reopened them. A greenish-gold glow burned across the pupils, painfully bright. She turned her head toward the area of the loft where she slept, and a moment later Flo's white-clad body floated up and out of her bed. Her shortened hair trailed downward a couple of inches, swaying in the currents of air across the loft as Willow turned her slowly and brought her over to where she stood, then lowered her until she floated about a foot off the ground.

"Let me show you," she intoned, "where Flo was sent. It is a place where each day feels like a year, each year like a century. What you will see here is what Flo remembers, the recollection that is branded permanently into her brain. I could have left her there, but I didn't." Willow cupped her palms, then swept them apart in the space over Flo's body, as though she were opening the curtains in front of a movie screen. They all stared open-mouthed at the scene that unfolded before them.

There was a lot of darkness, stark blackness sometimes cut by lighter gray shadows but never true daylight. It might have been a jungle or a pine tree forest—no one could quite tell. Unseen things whispered from every direction, shaking the branches and the foliage, rubbing up against her. The mottled darkness swayed and jerked, as if Flo had been twisting around constantly as she tried to keep track of whatever was stalking her . . . and there was *definitely* someone or some*thing* there, pacing her, pausing when she paused, turning and running and slowing, mimicking her every move.

A faster movement then, something quick and black sweeping across their view, enough to make them all jump and shudder. No one was sure, but it reminded them of oversized bat wings, mutated out of control. Or maybe dragons' wings, mythical things claimed to have existed, although no one had seen a dragon in recorded history. Black, potentially shapeless, it nevertheless gave the impression of teeth, rows and rows and rows of sharpened gray bone oozing anticipatory digestive fluids.

"There are places in the world," Willow said, her voice still hollow and far-away, "*our* world, where civilization has not caught up. Where man is predator not only of animals, but of his own kind, and where they have learned to twist magick to serve their own dark purposes. It's a place where the monsters in and out of your own mind cannot be outrun." Willow's eyes blazed even brighter. "And now that I've gathered a little more information, I *can* send the more adventurous of you to share in her experiences." She gave them a moment or two, then said, "In fact, to be fair, we'll give you *all* an equal preview!"

Willow's hands had been spread apart as if she still held back the invisible curtains. Suddenly she made a jerking motion with each one, and something unseen *ripped*—

And the loft surrounding them disappeared.

It was like being dropped into an abyss—there was a stomach-wrenching sensation of falling, then anything and everything civilized was replaced by utter primitive. Now around them there was only the jungle in the middle of the night, filled with greenery so lush and thick that it was nothing more than black and black-green blotches. Each of the women knew the others were there . . . *somewhere*, but that knowledge was no comfort. A turn one way and each one was lost, and they dared not cry out to try and find another of their own kind because they knew—each and every one of them instinctively and instantly knew—that they were all being hunted.

Flailing, gasping, seeing nothing until the screaming started, too many of them to count. Flashes of fire in the blackness, a sound like thunder or maybe the sharp crack of a lightning bolt—

—and Willow clapped her hands hard enough to make the skin on her palms sting.

The terrifying shadowland that still existed in Flo's mind and had surrounded all of them abruptly disappeared. Willow looked at them calmly, her eyes still shining with that hellish green glow. "It would only take a day of being there to make you all like Flo," she said. "To make you feel as though you had been trapped there for months on end. How do you think it would feel to be there . . . forever?"

Four of the twelve Wiccans had ended up curled into protective balls, while the others just sat and occasionally shuddered. Not a single one had come through the vision unimpressed, and that, Willow thought smugly, was a good thing. Sometimes the person in charge just needed to hit her underlings over the head with the obvious.

"You didn't have to do that," Amy snapped. There was a bloody streak down one arm where, during her fugue, she'd clawed at something she'd thought was on her skin. "I'm . . . *serving* you, or whatever you want to call it!"

Willow shook her head, then closed her eyes briefly and willed the churning energy inside her dissipate. "No, you're not." She motioned at Flo's body, still floating serenely above the floor. "Even like this, Flo serves me, channeling power for me should I require it, enabling me to tap into other realms if necessary. Never questioning, never balking. *That's* serving. In return I offer her nothing . . . but given the chance, I *will* grab the opportunity to restore her mind and repair her body." She looked around at the others, a number of whom were still twitching and sweating from their excursion into the unnamed location that had destroyed Flo's sanity. "No more questions," she said, and her tone made it clear that this time they'd better listen. The Ghost of Tara had once accused her of corrupting the other women, but so what? If she was, she was also empowering them, enabling them to finally achieve their full potential, offering them access to knowledge of the paths they might not have previously taken. But certain of those paths were off limits as of right now. "And no more rebellions. Think very hard before you cross me, because there *are* fates worse than death, and they don't always involve the demonic or vampiric. As you just saw, I can take you out one at a time—

"—or I can destroy all of you on a single whim."

"All right," Giles said, "the new version of the spell is ready." He held up a piece of paper, then offered it to Anya.

"What's that?" Dawn asked. "Coven Dispersion, version 2.0?"

"Definitely." Giles tapped the spell book he had balanced on his knees. It was a heavy thing with a crusted leather cover and metal buckles for hinges, but of course, he couldn't feel its weight. "What I've done is turn to ancient rituals combined with modern astrology to gain definitive location points. We're still going for the dispersion method, but this time—"

"No animals will be harmed in the making of this video?" Xander quipped. When no one laughed, he looked sheepish. "Sorry. Bad joke."

"While your career as a comedian may be short-lived," Giles said, "you're not far from the truth. I've taken an extreme amount of care to ensure that any of the Wiccans who are removed as a result of this spell end up in a safe place—no waiting devil tribes or cannibals, or anything remotely of that sort."

Xander peered at him. "Playing devil's advocate here, why, again, do we care about what happens to these evil witches?"

"Because they're just people, Xander," Giles said sternly. "Not vampires or demons. It's highly likely that being exposed to Willow the way she is now is playing a big factor in permanently contaminating their personalities. Before she pulled them into service, they might have been as good as anyone in this room."

"Wait," Dawn said. "Back up to the sending-away part. You said 'any' of them. How high on the doubt factor are you climbing here?"

"I'm not." Giles sounded absolutely convinced.

"I sure hope so. I'm not looking forward to another skydiving session out of Willow's window," Dawn retorted.

"Dawn has a point, Giles." Buffy folded her arms and regarded him. "Willow's gone heavy-hitter with the power scorecard, and a lot of that she got from you. Are you sure you're up to it?"

"Of course I am!" Giles said, sounding a little more defensive than he intended. "Besides, the entire spell has changed; you needn't worry about trying to get on the roof, and you certainly won't have to break through any windows. What I'm giving Anya now is a trio of spells. The first will open that door regardless of what kind of closure Willow has put on it. The second is a navigational incantation; it will literally put a light map on the floor for you. Follow it, and it will take you upstairs."

"And last but not least?" Xander prompted.

"The third is what you young people would call a super version of the previous dissolution spell." Giles lifted his chin proudly. "Better, bigger, faster, more powerful."

"All the things a man typically wants in a new toy," Anya noted wryly.

Xander had to nod. "So true."

"All right," Buffy said in a no-nonsense voice. "Then let's get to it."

Giles looked at his watch pointedly. "You have to go to work," he reminded her. "I don't think I need to mention how important it is that we keep up with the information flow on the street now that Willow has virtually taken over Sunnydale."

"Oh, no," Buffy said. "No way are you guys going over there without me. I'll just go in late or—"

"I know that guy you work for," Anya said. "What's his name?"

"Ash."

"Ash. Right. As a vengeance demon, I've had a lot of complaints about him. At least five women told me he fired them." She shrugged. "Too bad no one ever thought to wish against him. The man has the soul of a graveyard statue."

"Exactly my point," Giles said. "You *must* keep this job, Buffy."

Buffy looked decidedly unhappy. "I can find another one."

"Your ladder of success potential doesn't have a lot of rungs on it," Anya told her. "Think about it. You've gone from Doublemeat Palace to bar hop. Next stop—"

"Fine," Buffy said before Anya could finish. She really didn't want to hear what kind of creativity Anya's no-holds-barred brain could bring to the Buffy Career Suggestion Box. "But you guys be careful. And bail if it looks like anything's going wrong. We don't need anyone else to get hurt by Willow. We've got enough trouble with that right now." When they all stared at her, Buffy suddenly flushed red. "Okay, that didn't come out the way it should have. What I meant was—"

"Never mind," Giles said gruffly. "You didn't say anything not already in the minds of everyone else." He motioned at the door. "Go on, then. We'll meet you here after your shift."

With a last, unhappy glance at the rest of the gang, Buffy reluctantly headed off to the bar.

Chapter Seven

"**A**m I the only person having a really ugly déjà vu moment?" Xander glanced at the others. "The usual 'been there, done that' line seems just a mite too light."

"Trust me," Giles said, but there was a note of grimness in his voice. "This *will* work."

"I hope that's because of your great skill in hocus pocus and not just because you really, really want it to." Anya peered anxiously down the street from their spot a block from Willow's loft. She couldn't see much, just that same strangely oceanic pattern on the outside of the walls. She wondered what it meant. Did it have something to do with calmness? Was Willow trying to invoke a sense of peace around herself now? Anya had to admit that was kind of far-fetched. The whole evil coven and blue cat-demon thing really blew that idea out of the theoretical ocean anyway. She probably just liked blue.

As before, they couldn't see any lights on anywhere. All the broken windows had been repaired and were now fully camouflaged, all signs of a battle or that people had ever gone in and out had been entirely erased. Even the concrete sidewalk and the side parking areas had been swept clear of any loose debris, giving the impression that nothing had ever happened. In fact it looked even better than it had before. A line of multicolored, ornamental garden stones had been arranged along the bottom of the building, giving it a neat, professionally landscaped appearance. And no ugly brown stain marred the pavement where Willow's *sine kot diabl* had disintegrated and burned. The whole situation was nerve-wracking, and Anya now wished they'd loaded themselves down with weapons; they had a few things, but Giles had insisted that they'd likely not need them and pointed out that heavy metal would only slow them down.

"The door," Giles said. "Take me over there."

Without saying anything, Anya got behind the wheelchair and began pushing. It was so quiet, so dark, and Anya couldn't help being jumpy. Something was wrong here; it would have made much more sense for Willow to double or even triple the amount of security she had on her place, to have anything but the dead silence and stillness that permeated everything. With a start, Anya realized that she was having trouble breathing deeply; instead she was taking in short, quiet gasps, a reaction that only happened when she was truly afraid and trying to hide from something.

But there was nothing here.

Was there?

The distance to the door of Willow's building felt more like a mile than a block. The noise that the wheels on Giles's chair made as they grated over the concrete was obnoxiously loud, splitting the darkness like an unwanted announcement of their arrival. When they finally got to the door, the building loomed ominously over them, as though it had somehow added fifty feet to its normal two-story height.

"Something's not right," Dawn said suddenly. "This is way too easy."

"Yeah," Xander agreed. "After the way we busted up her place the last time, I can't believe Willow would just let us waltz right up to the front entrance like this."

"Perhaps she's simply overconfident," Giles suggested, but there was an undertone to his voice that suggested he was grasping.

"Well, she does have that attitude thing going," Anya said, but she didn't sound at all convinced.

"Then let's hurry it up," Xander said. "My fingers and various other body parts are crossed that she's not even home right now."

Dawn rolled her eyes. "And what are the odds of that? I bet she's in there just waiting for—"

Her words broke off as something huge and dark lumbered toward them from around the corner of the building.

"Giles, what the hell is *that*?" Xander's voice rose until the last word was soaked with panic.

Giles twisted on his chair so he could squint past Xander, but he couldn't quite see. "I'm not sure," he said.

"Uh," Dawn said shakily, "whatever it is, it's headed straight for us. And I'm pretty sure it's not human."

There was precious little light around, most of it from a single streetlight about twenty feet too far away. The creature heading toward them was taller than Xander and quite a bit more stocky. It was shaped like a man, and yet . . . not really—its lines were too straight and undetailed, its movements more clumsy than natural. It wasn't particularly fast, but it wasn't turtle slow, either.

"What do you think?" Xander sucked in a deep breath, then moved in front of Giles's chair and pulled a black metal rod off his belt. Called an extendable baton, a flick of his wrist made it extend to three times its length. It wasn't as good as a big sharp blade, but as defenses went, it was better than bare knuckles and it ought to give an attacker a heck of a sore spot or three.

Anya gripped the handles of Giles's wheelchair and began pulling him backward. "Oh, no," she said. "Oh, no no no." Her gaze was locked on the creature moving in their direction, and it was closing the distance far too quickly. "We have to get out of here. This doesn't look so good, and I really think we need to leave before—"

Too late.

The thing covered the final five feet a lot faster than Xander had anticipated. Xander swung his baton, but he was about a second and a half too late; what connected with the creature's arm was his wrist—the thing had already stepped inside the arc of his swing. It was like hitting concrete, and the impact sent a jolt all the way up his arm to his shoulder. "Ow," Xander said reflexively.

For a half an instant, Xander and the creature stared at each other. Then it wrapped one rough, over-sized hand around his neck, picked him up, and easily tossed him out of its way.

"Golem!" Giles suddenly screamed. *"Run!"*

Anya yanked Giles backward as the gray-colored creature grabbed for him, and she barely got Giles out of its reach in time. Gritting her teeth, Dawn ducked under the golem's heavy, outstretched arm, turned sideways, and put her shoulder into a push that had her full body weight in it. Unfortunately the creature didn't budge and all she got for her effort was a blank-eyed stare from the thing. She had time to be surprised that it had hazel eyes, then it shoved her aside with the same noneffort it had shown with Xander. That done, it fastened its gaze on the next person closest to it.

Giles.

Even though he was only a few feet away, the librarian held up a hand, as if he wanted to stop Anya from pulling him out of range. He leaned forward almost eagerly, straining to see the golem's features. "Anya, wait. There's writing on it, and something else about this thing that's famil—"

There was no time for this. Anya snarled and spun Giles's around to face the other direction, putting her-self between the golem and the wheelchair-bound man. Everyone was yelling at once, with too much overlap in the words to understand any single sentence.

"Go!" she screamed at Giles, and at the same time she morphed into her stronger vengeance demon form. *"Get out of here NOW!"* Without waiting for an answer, she shoved Giles's wheelchair forward with as much strength as she could muster, then realized in dismay that it had been too much. She had a single, regret-filled second to watch the librarian career about ten feet before the chair tipped over and the paralyzed man spilled onto the concrete. Splayed in two different spots, Xander and Dawn were still picking themselves up and were too far away to help.

Anya started toward him automatically, then something hard tangled in her hair and pulled her back. "Hey—*ow!* Let go of me, you thick-headed piece of dried dirt!"

The golem didn't obey. Instead it spun her around and smacked her hard across the face. Anya screeched and hit it back, her demon-based strength enough to at least make an impact. It grunted and released her hair, but she didn't get out of the way fast enough to avoid getting whacked again across the same cheekbone.

Coming in low and from behind, Xander wielded his baton like a metal baseball bat and began pounding energetically on the golem's lower legs. The golem roared in anger and spun to face him, legs shaking with each blow; still, the bulky creature refused to go down. Dawn got her hand around one of the colored rocks at the side of the building; she stretched up and beat on the side of the golem's head with it, but the only result was that it turned its unwanted attention to her rather than Xander. Spitting blood out of the side of her mouth, Anya leaped on the creature's back, curled her fingers into claws, and went for its eyes.

Three yards away, Giles was on his side on the ground with the wheelchair upended nearly three feet away. All he could do was try to get over there to it, force it upright, then drag himself into it. Beyond that . . . not much. Beyond the items he'd intended to use upstairs in Willow's loft, he'd foolishly not brought any spell books or other weapons with him, and the last thing he'd been expecting here was a golem; none of the spells he could think of in his head at the moment would have any effect on the elemental creature.

Utterly humiliated, indescribably angry, the one-time Watcher used his arms to drag himself along the ground toward his wheelchair. The rough pavement scratched into the palms of his hands, and no doubt his knees and legs were getting the same dosage. Of course, the way things were going, a few scraped and grit-filled patches of skin might not be the only injuries he'd come away with.

With three people on top of it, by the time Giles managed to right his wheelchair and pull himself into it, the golem had had enough. It roared and flung its arms wide, dislodging Dawn with one hand and back-punching Anya brutally in the eye with its other. Dawn went sliding across the sidewalk with a wail as the concrete burned into the flesh of her left arm; at the same time, Anya's head snapped backward with enough force to make her lose her hold and *thunk* hard to the ground. She would have sat there, stunned, had Xander not knocked her out of the way and taken his baton blows up higher, this time aiming for the golem's face. He thwacked it once, then twice. His third swing was stopped short by the golem's rock hard forearm; then, just to make it clear he was annoyed, the golem folded its arm and pulled it in to its body, only to shoot its elbow back out . . . right into Xander's nose.

Xander toppled over and, even with one hand clamped over his now-gushing nose, fought the urge to curl into a ball and pass out. A distant part of him thought he might as well, because he certainly couldn't see; the pain across the bridge of his nose was so great that his eyes had squeezed shut and no amount of mental commands would make them reopen. Ultimately, the best he could do was to spin in a sort of drunken crouch, one hand cupped over his nose while the other one waved wildly somewhere in front of his head.

"Xander, come on!"

Xander twisted toward the sound of Giles's voice and stumbled forward. He went down on one knee but didn't feel it when his skin collided with the concrete. His nose, or what was left of it, was everything right now, an all-encompassing cloud of pain and pretty much all he could think about. That he could even hear Giles's voice was an accomplishment in itself.

"Anya, get him and Dawn and let's get out of here!"

Hands grabbed him by each arm and propelled him forward. It had to be the two women, and because he still couldn't see them, Xander had no choice but to trust his unseen rescuers, to go where they were dragging him. There was a low blustering in the background that his mind registered as the golem's threatening sound, but it faded bit by bit as he tottered along between Dawn and Anya—praise everything that could be praised, apparently the mud man had decided it wasn't worth it to follow them. Something hit him across the hips—the back of Giles's wheelchair—and then he was sandwiched neatly between it, Anya, and Dawn, and they were rushing as fast as they could away from the Willow's building and her golem.

"Oh, th-that was just g-great!" Dawn cried. Her voice jounced every time her forward run put her left leg down and it wanted to buckle. Her left arm felt like it was on fire. "Trust me, he says, this will work!"

"Thuddub," Xander managed to say. He could barely breathe and he felt like someone had stuffed the world's biggest, spike-studded feather pillow inside his nose and sinuses. Every step made a bass drum go off behind his eyes. "Jus' . . . thud*dub*."

"Be quiet, both of you," Anya hissed. She was still in demon mode, pulling them along on the extra strength, wanting to put as much distance as possible between them and the golem. "We'll be lucky if that thing doesn't follow us back to the Magic Box!"

"We have to get there as quickly as possible," Giles said. "Once inside, if it's following us, I can do a spell to lock it out, at least for a couple of hours. It won't wait around—they're rather mindless creations. It will want to go back to its creator."

Anya chanced a look over her shoulder, but thankfully the golem wasn't chasing them. She could see it, standing back by Willow's building like a big, dumb statue. "I think we're okay," she told him. "It's staying back there."

They traveled the rest of the way back to the Magic Box in silence, with Anya finally letting herself slip back to human mode as they made it to the door. Inside, they assessed the damage, and it wasn't good.

Giles had gotten off easy. A little road rash along his palms was really about the extent of it, although none of the others could have had any idea just how completely degraded he felt. Sitting there quietly after wiping his hands with alcohol, he relished the burn of his flesh as self-punishment while he watched the others attend to their wounds; he listened to the occasional bickering of the other three with only a minimum of attention, fighting the whole time not to sink into a puddle of self-pity. Their injuries were nothing to be scoffed at, especially Xander's, and Giles blamed himself for this; while he still believed all three of his new spells would have worked without a hitch, he despised himself for not having had the foresight to know that something like this was inevitable.

How idiotic had he been to think Willow would focus on strengthening spells that had already failed to keep them out? Foolish, indeed. In hindsight, it made total sense that she would devise a different plan, something with much more impact, to guard her home ground. She'd already shown that she was quite adept at calling up demons with the creation of her *sine kot diabl*, but because that creature had existed solely to funnel power into her, Giles had somehow in his own mind downplayed her capabilities. Perhaps subconsciously he simply hadn't wanted to believe that the old and still-loved Willow had changed into someone who would do something that might seriously, intentionally cause them harm. Obviously she could and she would. Of course, hindsight was always twenty-twenty, and lately Giles was starting to think he was operating with blinders glued to the front of his skull.

But there sure wouldn't be anything blind about Buffy when she came home from her night's work and saw the results of their failed attempt—make that their second failed attempt—at disarming Willow's coven.

Chapter Eight

"*Miss Summers.*"

Buffy pressed her lips together, then turned to meet the face that went with the familiar voice. "You again," she said. "You know, can't a tired Slayer just head home from work without being bothered by strangers?" Flippant talk on the surface, but she still had the mark of this beast's whip across her cheek as a reminder of their last encounter. It was almost healed, but the tenseness in her jaw now made it give her a painful throb. She'd kept his two whips and added them to the arsenal stored at the Magic Box, but there was no guarantee he didn't have another duo stashed in the folds of the black gi he wore tonight, having left the more modern garb of jeans and jacket behind in favor of tradition. Now that she thought about it, the gi had enough material to it so that he might conceal anything from a Japanese Katana to an old-fashioned Mr. Pointy of his own. Why couldn't he have stuck with the black jeans?

The vampire inclined his head respectfully. "My apologies, but we have unfinished business."

"Make an appointment," Buffy said, but she made no move to leave. "The new vamps in town have to get in line to die."

His black, black eyes glittered. "I am the only one who counts. By your death, I will rule the others."

Buffy shot him a look that was half disgusted, half disbelieving. "My, aren't you just riding the ego-coaster?"

He shrugged but never took his eyes off her. "It is well known that you are no longer the Slayer you once were, that the new Wiccan queen has, shall we say, dulled the point of your stakes. There are those who believe your time is over and my own kind should take their rightful place in the food web of this town. I am one of them."

"You *are* new in town," Buffy marveled. "Otherwise you'd know that the food web around here does *not* want me tangled in it. I tend to tear the strings."

"Then it is clearly time for you to travel the path of your demise."

Buffy sniggered. "Path of my demise? What century did you come out of, anyway?"

He smiled. "It is only proper that you know the name of the man who is about to kill you," he said. "Although it will do you no good, at the end of your time, when you beg for mercy, you may call me Jaw-long Shing Yu."

Buffy's eyes narrowed. Her Slayer-sense was kicking in—Mr. Conversation here was about to attack. "That's quite a mouthful," she said. She let the last syllable sound like she was going to say something further, but she didn't. Rather than continue the small talk or wait for his reply—and whatever bad was coming with it—she dove for his legs.

She missed, but that was okay, because so did he. A double dose of something black and metallic whizzed right through where her head had been only an instant before; she had a breath's time to register the six-pointed ninja throwing stars lodged deeply in the metal door of a van parked at the curb, then the two of them were in full grapple mode on the sidewalk.

Once, in what felt oddly like someone else's lifetime, Buffy had battled a beautiful vampire named Celina, a woman who'd been born first as Cassia in sixteenth-century Greece. A turned Slayer herself, Celina had very nearly killed Buffy not once, but twice, and although the second time—when Buffy had ultimately triumphed—Celina had used mind tricks on her, the first had been more physical, and more reality-based brutal. Endowed with ancient Slayer skills and a vampire's strength, Celina had lived long enough to spend time in Europe and the far east, mastering a dozen martial arts for which Buffy didn't even have a name. The memory had left Buffy with experience and a great respect—and dread—for the beasties of the underworld who knew about such things. That she hadn't quite defeated Celina on her own—Willow, Tara, and Dawn had added a little *oomph!* to the

Slayage pot with a blessing spell—was a secret embarrassment that made Buffy all the more cautious.

Perhaps Jaw-long was younger than Celina had been, or maybe he'd simply followed a different course of study. Whatever the reason, he couldn't quite get the hold on her that Celina had managed to maintain in Buffy's battles with her; every time he thought he was progressing into a position of dominance, Buffy turned the tables and he found himself on the defensive again.

At one point he maneuvered to pull something out of his pocket, then hit her in the head with it so hard he nearly knocked her senseless. She went on autopilot for the second or two it took her to recuperate, and when he pulled back to try to twirl the nunchaku again, Jaw-long gave Buffy just enough room to hit him so hard across the throat with her forearm that he gagged and fell backward.

Buffy wasn't about to look back on this movement and think she was foolish for not following him. Jaw-long was a formidable enough opponent so that if she didn't, she might not live long enough to review her mistakes. She let her body weight flow with his, landing full-length on top of him, face-to-face. He had one moment to be surprised as he stared into her eyes—

—then Buffy thumped onto the pile of dust on the ground where Jaw-long Shing Yu used to be.

She'd learned a long time ago that a Slayer and a vampire always needed to have something come between them if they fell together.

Spitting dust and brushing herself off, Buffy got to her feet and peered around the darkened street, half convinced that some samurai-sword wielding buddy of Jaw-long's would leap from behind one of the cars. When no one did, she backed away from the pile of dust and headed to the Magic Box, thinking about what the vampire had said. It wasn't the part about how she could beg for mercy before she died—like *that* would ever happen—but the observation about her Slayerness. What had he said?

"It is well known that you are no longer the Slayer you once were, that the new Wiccan queen has, shall we say, dulled the point of your stakes."

Just the notion that this might be true was enough to make Buffy's face flush with shame and embarrassment. Okay, so maybe it was true that Willow was in kick-ass victory mode right now, and maybe she *had* trounced Buffy a couple of times, but was that such a big deal that every scuzzball out-of-town vampire saw it as an invitation to suddenly try to rule the roost? Were they really that convinced that she was no longer the vampires' main problem in town—that she was all washed up?

A bad thing to think about, even in the wake of a victory, because it put her mood way in the realm of black.

And walking into the Magic Box to find her sister and all her friends practically pounded to pulpness sure didn't give her the happy she needed to pull out of it.

"So what happened to simply waving that dragon's blood all around?" demanded Buffy. "Giles, *look* at them. Did you see Dawn's arm? And Xander's nose? And—"

"I'm not blind, Buffy," Giles said irritably. "I'm well aware of their injuries. In fact, I helped minister to them."

"Great," muttered Buffy. She stared at Xander, but he seemed too miserable to notice. Both of his eyes were circled with black and the deep red-purple of severe bruising. His nose was puffed up and swollen to three times its normal size, splayed across his face as though someone had smashed it flat with a hammer. He wanted to tell Buffy that was exactly how it felt, except it hurt too damned much to talk.

"Stob looging ad me," Xander finally ventured. His voice was stuffy and thick with pain, but they could still understand his words. "I'm da vigdum, rebember?"

Buffy sighed, then turned her attention to Dawn. The teenager was almost as bad as Xander, but in a different way. One arm was scraped nearly to the bone where she'd slid across the surface of the concrete, the speed of her body turning her skin into a human scouring pad. The result was a red and open wound that oozed blood and was much too raw to even wrap a bandage around. Dawn was gamely trying to be brave, but Buffy could tell there was major pain involved.

Even Anya hadn't gotten off free. From the story they'd relayed to Buffy, Anya's demon mode had probably saved her a thrashing as bloody and painful as Xander's and Dawn's. Even so, one cheekbone was heavily bruised and showed a three-inch cut.

As far as Buffy could tell, only Giles, wheelchair-bound and nearly helpless, seemed to have escaped without injury. He might have a few bumps and bruises under his clothes, but the sad fact was that from the waist down, he wouldn't have a clue. It was the others who'd been pancaked trying to keep him safe, and it infuriated Buffy that they'd gone through all that, yet never even had a chance to start reading the first of the three spells. Was Willow really getting that seriously strong? Or was Giles just as seriously falling down on his end of the Wiccan-repellant team?

"Giles—"

"Buffy, there's something you need to know," Giles interrupted in a low voice. "If you'll just put your anger behind you for a moment."

"What?" Buffy asked crankily. "More news flash about what a bad deal Willow is? I got that edition, remember? Read it from cover to cover."

Giles took a deep breath. "Actually, it's about the golem. I think I know who it is."

Buffy stared at him, trying to process this. "Wait—*who* it is? Since when do men made of dirt actually *become* someone in particular?"

Giles looked down at the book he'd been studying, then flipped through a few pages of his own notes. "Rarely, but it does happen. While we were waiting for you to get home—"

"And licking our wounds," Anya threw in bitingly.

"—I researched it thoroughly. It takes not only a thorough knowledge of the black arts, which Willow has, but a spirit new to the spiritual realm and which hasn't yet decided to pass on. That spirit must also be drawn to the ritual somehow, either by familiarity with the necromancer performing it, a desire to return to or stay in the area, or both." He looked at Buffy gravely. "If I'm correct in my assessment and in what I saw earlier tonight, it seems Willow found herself the perfect cooperative spirit."

"Well, we certainly lose enough bodies around here on a regular basis," Buffy said. "Since we've already seen Tara floating around here on her own, just who has Willow ectoplasmically inserted into tall, dark, and dirty?"

"Riley Finn."

Silence.

Finally Buffy blinked, then frowned at Giles. "Excuse me, I thought you said Riley."

"I did," he said softly.

Buffy swallowed. "But, Giles . . . that would mean he's dead."

"I'm afraid so."

"I *thought* those hazel eyes looked familiar." Anya's voice was just a little too loud, but the volume failed to disguise her shock.

"But he was . . . he was fine not so long ago." Buffy turned toward Dawn, as if her sister could somehow help support her argument. "He was here, in Sunnydale, with his wife, remember? They were fine, really fine." She extended a hand toward the others. "I mean, you guys saw them, right? They were in love, and . . . and . . ." Her words died away for a moment. "Riley . . . he can't be dead. Can he?"

Giles rubbed his temple. "I know what I saw, Buffy.

I *recognized* his features in the face of that creature." He tapped his notes thoughtfully. "Just to be on the safe side, so there are no doubts whatsoever, I suggest you make a few telephone calls." He fixed her with a serious look. "You were able to reach the Initiative before with the number that Riley left. They might be able tell you what you need to know."

"Or not," Dawn said. "I don't recall them being particularly cooperative about giving up the info."

"It's worth a try," Buffy said, and they could all hear the misery in her voice. "I'll . . . be back."

The training room was the one area of the Magic Box that hadn't been rebuilt. Now it was full of dust and splintered wood; broken pieces and parts of weapons lay like the remnants of a lost war. Xander had promised he would rebuild it as he had the rest of the shop, but it was one of those someday things that he was supposed to get to. Buffy thought that "someday" was a word that ought to be banned from the English language, or maybe just deleted altogether, as though it had never existed to begin with. In reality, saying that something was going to get done "someday" was nothing but another way of saying "never."

Someday she would get to finish college.

Someday she would have a career, a job that didn't mean taking orders for fries and fake-meat burgers, or serving high-dose alcohol to dirty bikers and back-street low-level demons.

Someday she would learn to drive a car without

scaring three years off the life of anyone in the passenger seat. Okay, maybe that was a long shot, but again, it was another someday.

Someday she'd have a relationship with a normal man, get married, and have babies, like the mega-percentage of other women in the world.

Yeah, right. And wasn't *that* one just the biggest "someday" of them all?

Riley Finn.

She thought about him—how could she not?—as she dialed a certain number and listened to the phone ring in a place somewhere in the world that she couldn't guess.

Buffy had come so close to that last "someday" with him, or at least, for a while she'd allowed herself to think she might. Passion, love—or so she'd believed—and this time she'd received more than she'd given. He'd left her believing she didn't love him, didn't need him; she had, but the realization of that had sunk into her thick Slayer skull too late to save their relationship. The pain of watching his helicopter take off into the black of the night had been magnified a hundredfold just recently when he'd returned with his wife, Sam. Buffy had run the gamut there—jealousy, desire, regret—but ultimately she'd had no choice but to accept the new fact that Riley loved his wife and off they would go to live happily ever after.

Not.

The cell phone clicked in her hand and she realized that her call was being rerouted, probably more than once. Finally, a voice on the other end. Cold, distant, sexless.

"Yes."

"This is Buffy Summers," she said clearly. "I'm calling . . . I'm calling because I've received some information about Riley Finn. I wanted to make sure it wasn't true."

Silence then, long enough so that she began to wonder if she'd lost the connection. But no—there was someone there, she could feel it. She could play the waiting game as long as necessary. Finally the disembodied voice came back through the earpiece, giving her a question but totally without cadence.

"What information."

"I-I—" For a moment, Buffy couldn't make herself speak the words. "I've been told that he's dead."

The pause this time wasn't as long.

"Yes."

The room spun crazily for a second, then Buffy put a hand against the wall and found a measure of stability. "H-how?" she asked, not even knowing if the voice would tell her. "When? Does his wife kn—"

"Dead."

"Oh."

"They were killed in Nepal a week ago by a firewing."

The muscles along Buffy's neck tightened. A firewing? What the hell was *that?* The voice cut her off before she could form her next question. *"That's all the information available."*

Click.

Buffy stared into space with the telephone still pressed against her ear.

"It's true."

Three shocked faces turned toward Buffy as she gave them the bitter news. "True?" Dawn repeated in a small voice. "Riley's really dead?"

Buffy nodded. She'd given herself a few minutes to deal with it in private, but there was no way to hide the telltale signs of crying. "His wife, too. They were killed by something called a firewing." She swallowed. "It happened in Nepal," she added. "That's all they would tell me. 'They' being a voice on the phone."

Xander looked at Buffy, then at the floor. "Thad suggs," he said. It was only the second time she'd heard him talk since finding out he had a broken nose; by the looks of it, just those two words were painful.

"I'm so sorry, Buffy," Giles said.

Dawn said nothing, but the tears streaming down her cheeks revealed how upset she was. When Riley and her sister had been an item, she'd resented Riley mightily sometimes because of the attention her sister had lavished on him, how she'd often felt locked out of her sister's affection. But she'd also secretly empathized with him, especially at the end when it had become so apparent to everyone but Buffy how far at arm's length she was keeping him (and everyone else), how they all played second fiddle to her Slayerness. She could so understand how Riley had felt when Buffy was always the faster, stronger one, always saving others and never wanting him to come along because he might get hurt and she didn't want to have to save him, too. How completely and utterly *unnecessary* he'd felt. It didn't seem fair that not long after he'd finally found someone who thought he was the most important thing in the world, the two of them had been killed.

Anya frowned. "Did you say firewing?"

Buffy nodded. "Yeah. I . . . hope that's not as bad as it sounds."

Anya's expression darkened. "I don't think you want to know." She paused, then added, "At least it was probably fast."

Giles looked at his useless legs, then glanced away. "I suppose that's all any of us could hope for."

No one spoke for a long time, then Giles finally cleared his throat. "I realize it's difficult to take, but we'll have to deal with this."

Buffy sank into one of the chairs. "I don't get it. What good would it do to put Riley's spirit into a plodding mud-puppet, anyway? I mean, golems are just kind of . . . *there*, right? They don't have much brainpower or anything. They can't *think*. They just fight."

"Well," Giles said, "according to some of the more arcane texts, that's not altogether accurate. A golem with a spirit inserted into it can prove quite useful, especially when given orders related to a person upon whom the golem's spirit fixated in its life."

Xander looked from Giles to Buffy, then back again. "Uh-oh."

"Indeed," Giles said. "I'd venture to say that Willow is counting on feelings of bitterness that may have been buried in Riley's subconscious to help 'fuel' him, if you will, should it actually encounter you face to face. Because of that, I'd strongly recommend you avoid it."

Buffy shrugged, but remembering how hurt Riley had been at the end of their relationship didn't make her feel nearly as confident as the movement implied. "So what? It's just a man made of dirt."

"Hardly." Giles gave the book on his lap a sharp tap. "Golems are *extremely* dangerous, Buffy, as if what that creature did to Xander, Anya, and Dawn isn't enough evidence of that. To complicate matters further, as a combination of earthen and demonic creation, they are very nearly impervious to magic. One with a spirit incorporated into it is not only rare, but even more of a threat because of its focus."

Buffy inhaled deeply. "Okay. How do I kill it?"

"Wait," Dawn said, suddenly sitting up straight. "If you kill it, aren't you going to hurt Riley's spirit, or soul, or whatever that is inside it?"

Giles shook his head. "No. If anything, you'll release it, and that can only be a good thing. As for killing a golem, the ability to do so directly depends on the golem itself and how it was created. I do recall seeing writing on the thing's forehead, and while I didn't have a chance to actually read what it said, there are only a few sayings that will animate a golem. Depending on what's written there, we need only erase all or a part of it."

"Great," Anya said. "It's only about seven feet tall. We'll just ask it to lean over and stand still for a moment."

"Oh, I'll erase it, all right," Buffy said grimly.

Giles shook his finger at her. "No, you won't, at least not by yourself. Erase the wrong word and you may well make it completely indestructible."

Buffy's mouth worked, but all she finally said was, "Oh."

"And there's more," Giles added.

"Bunderbul," Xander said. There was an ice pack lying on a plate, and he picked it up and gingerly pressed it to the bridge of his nose. "Ow."

"I find it highly unlikely that Willow, given her extensive knowledge of the black arts, would bring her golem to life using only one method. My guess is she energized it with a second method, something a little better hidden. We'll have to find and remove *both* methods."

"Okay," Buffy said. "What's the second one? And how do we get rid of it?"

But Giles only looked at her and the others. "I have no idea."

Chapter Nine

It was quiet, dark, and finally empty of everyone save Willow, Spike, and Oz. And, of course, the ever-present Ghost of Tara.

Willow had sent the rest of the coven home, finally releasing them after a grueling eight-hour stretch of research and small, power-gathering spells. As a town, Sunnydale was slowly being sucked dry of its power sources, and Willow was thankful for the silent, trudging presence of the golem downstairs. Her Wiccans were the gatherers of the harvest for her, and even if they only grudgingly gave their services and obeyed her, they knew they were both protected by her and for her—no one else dared touch them. By the same token, with everything and everyone else in Sunnydale slowly being drained of supernatural energy, finding suitable replacements for these women should Giles try again and be successful would really be a challenge.

Successful? Fat chance, thanks to the golem. During the daylight hours the mud-man would back against the outside wall to blend in with her daytime camouflage enchantment. That didn't mean he was powerless during the day—far from it. There were no sunrise or sunset restrictions on his wrath.

Feeling more secure than she had ever since she'd walked in and found Buffy traipsing uninvited around the loft, Willow lit candles all around the huge room, relaxing a little with each soft glow that rose from the candlewicks, each scented with herb that mingled with the one before it. In only a few minutes, the loft was filled with warm, golden light, each candle flame flickering gently on the natural drafts from the massive windows. It made everything around her seem more cozy and gentle, almost like a real home.

Except there was no Tara, of course.

"I'm here, Willow."

Willow lit the last candle, then turned toward the sound of the spirit's soft voice. So beautiful, the blond hair and blue eyes, the full, sweet lips, and flawless skin. If only the sight of her beloved wasn't always marred by the bloodstained blouse. If only she wasn't just a shade too . . . see-through.

If only she were real.

There were plenty of "real" things around, and although she knew the Ghost of Tara meant to comfort her, there was precious little comfort in her life nowadays. Instead Willow's day-to-day existence seemed like it was filled with threats that came from every direction—Buffy, Giles, her unwilling Wiccans, and sometimes the monsters of her own creation. Even her pets had to be watched; in his perpetual werewolf state, Oz would kill her or anything else that got within his reach, and who could tell *what* the supposedly insane Spike might do? They'd certainly seen Angel do the Sybil-routine several times.

But tonight . . . tonight was okay. She was as secure in her own home as she could possibly make herself, and almost alone. Tonight she would concentrate on the nitty-gritty components she would need to resurrect Tara—the *real* Tara.

Willow had gathered together a number of spell books, an interesting combination of new and old. Read each one separately and a modern Wiccan might come up with the same conclusion that the Ghost of Tara kept insisting on: Willow would not be able to bring her back.

But Willow was not so easily deceived. She was used to reading between the lines, to finding the interpretations that other people missed—as had, for instance, several members of her own coven.

She'd caught the reference a couple of times and noted that no one else had bothered to follow up on it. She could almost understand it—in Wicca, they were used to dealing with Osiris and the Egyptian end of things. Unfortunately sometimes the lesser experienced tended to think that was the only way, when Mother Earth was full of possibilities.

Such as Yama, the Hindu God of Death.

Most people, when they thought about the darker history of India, immediately remembered the goddess Kali. But Hindu history was also full of tales about the princess Savitri. These fables ranged from her outwitting the dark-hearted Yama to straight-on doing battle with him and winning. But no matter how simple or far-fetched the story, the ending always remained the same: Savitri was granted the return of her husband's life when he was destined, by all accounts, to die less than one year after they'd met.

All of Willow's research had pushed her to a single, final conclusion: If Osiris would not listen to her, Willow would have to fight Yama, the God of Death, to win the right to bring Tara back from the dead.

It wasn't going to be easy. Bringing back Buffy hadn't been easy, either. Urns of Osiris weren't easy to come by, and frankly, she wasn't the deer hunter type—killing that fawn had taken a heavy hit of iron will driven by pure determination and stubbornness. Those things Willow still had, but did she have the strength to fight something as formidable as a god?

Well . . .

Yes, she did, damn it. Buffy had beaten Glory, and no matter what her Slayer abilities were, she had *not* had the go-power that Willow did now—she couldn't even come close. Combine Willow's current capacity with a little more help from the women of the coven and the right spell, and—

"It will never happen, Willow."

Willow jerked in surprise, then shot an exasperated

look at the Ghost of Tara. "Are you *trying* to make me mess up?" she demanded. "Stop sneaking up on me!"

The Ghost of Tara tilted her head, and for a heart-breaking moment Willow thought she saw a hint of Tara's humor there. But no—it was just wishful thinking, because when the Ghost of Tara spoke again, there was nothing amused about her words or her tone. *"It's futile, Willow. There is no benefit to my silence. I cannot help you accomplish what will never be allowed."*

Willow turned back to the spell book in front of her. "I don't believe that," she said. "If everyone let themselves be so limited by what other people told them, mankind would still think they'd fall off the edge of a flat world if they sailed too far on the ocean."

"True," the Ghost of Tara agreed. *"But we aren't talking pre-Christopher Columbus times and big ships here. We're talking forces with which you shouldn't be messing."*

Willow shrugged. "Really? Maybe you should remind yourself to take a long, hard look at Sunnydale. I think it's way too late for that kind of a limitation."

"This goes beyond that and you know it."

"You are too limited in your thinking," Willow told her. "Expand your mind set and let yourself consider *all* the possibilities . . . including ones that might not have been tried before. The methodology says—"

"Mythology."

Willow frowned. "What was that?"

"Mythology," the Ghost of Tara repeated. *"There's a difference—one that you're choosing to ignore."*

Willow raised an eyebrow. "You're wrong, in more

ways than one. First of all, I'm not ignoring anything.
I'm just not letting my success depend on your little
prophecies of doom and gloom. Secondly, can you say
that any of this"—she gestured at Spike and Oz, and
then at all the spellbooks and magickal paraphernalia
around her—"represents more than what most of the
world believes is myth? Look at Oz. To most people,
the way he is now is nothing but an old black-and-
white horror film. And vampires?" She rolled her eyes.
"Puh-leeze. Ask about that and the average Joe will tell
you it's a pallid Tom Cruise in a movie made from an
Anne Rice book."

"You think so?" The Ghost of Tara wandered
closer, making Willow wince slightly as the spirit
walked through the corner of a worktable rather than
around it—another reason why Willow couldn't think
of her as just Tara. *"I think you underestimate the
people in this town, although I don't guess it really
matters."* The spirit seemed as if she were studying the
books on the table, then she raised her gaze to Willow's. *"What you want to do defies the laws of the universe,"* she said. *"It won't be allow—"*

"How many times do we need to have this conversation?" Willow interrupted. It was an effort to
keep the sharpness out of her voice, and she had to
bite her tongue hard enough to make her eyes sting
before she could stop the rest of what she wanted to
say from coming out. She was just so tired of hearing
this defeatist attitude, this face-in-the-dirt, can't-
possibly-do-it motif. Was this what death had done to
Tara? Made her morose and sad and pessimistic? If

so, Willow sure hoped she'd leave all that in the coffin once Willow got her back.

Now the Ghost of Tara folded her hands in front of her solemnly, and with a jolt, Willow noticed for the first time that there was blood under two of her fingernails. *"I suppose we'll have this conversation until you accept that you can't possibly succeed."*

"No," Willow said. "That's not how it is at all." She lifted her chin, feeling stronger as she watched the first warm light of dawn break into the room. "We'll have it until I finally succeed and you realize that this time, about this mondo-big thing, you're absolutely, utterly wrong."

Chapter Ten

"Okay, everyone. I need some time," Anya announced.

Giles, sitting on his wheelchair behind the other side of the table, didn't even look up from the tome he was studying. "Of course, Anya," he murmured. "Take all the time you need."

"Time is good," Xander said enthusiastically. "We could go on a vacation. You know, I don't think we've ever done that." The smile he aimed at Anya was wide and bright. "It's not like things ever change much around here, anyway. Hellmouth, good and evil, fight and sometimes lose, go back until we win. It's not like it'll go away while we're gone."

"Xander, that's not what I'm talking about," Anya said. "What I meant was—"

"I think he's right," Dawn said. "We're not that far

from Los Angeles. You could drive there and take one of those cruises that leaves from Ports O' Call."

"I think those are pretty expensive," Buffy said.

"They don't have to be," Dawn told her. "They have ones that only go for three days, and if you book last minute, you can get really low-buck deals. I saw them online." She turned back to Anya. "Think of it. Three days of all-you-can-eat buffets, the big blue ocean, and the unblocked Cancun sun. No vampire would dare bother you."

"Right," Giles said absently. "Marvelous idea."

"Excuse me," Anya said loudly. "Can we get back on track? Could I actually have your *attention*?"

This time, Giles raised his head. "Of course, Anya," he said again.

At least this time he was actually looking at her. It was the least he could do considering what she was about to say.

"I've written a spell," she said simply. "And I need all of you to help me make it work."

Buffy frowned. "A spell? What kind of spell?"

Anya took a deep breath, then lifted her chin. "I'm going to make Giles walk again."

Not surprisingly, all jaws in the room fell open. Then they all started talking at once.

"What is it, a regeneration spell?" Giles asked in amazement.

"That's awesome!" Dawn exclaimed. "When can we start?"

"Say, are you sure this isn't going to do more harm than good?" asked Xander. "It's not going to mutate him into some kind of demon or something, is it?"

"I don't think this is a good idea," Buffy said. "This sounds like you're getting in way over your head, and if it has anything to do with the black arts, there's no way we're going through with it."

"Do you think it will work?" Giles asked excitedly. He plucked whatever he'd been reading from his lap along with the notes he'd been making and pushed them aside in a surprisingly untidy pile. "How does it go? What special ingredients do you need?"

"I'll help," Dawn said. "You want me to dig up some roots or something? I'm all for getting my hands muddy in this. Even my elbows."

"Wait," Xander said. "The whole spell thing really makes me nervous. I mean, we don't have a really good history with stuff like that and—"

"Be quiet!"

Xander gulped away the rest of his sentence and they all stared at Anya. She looked angrier than any of them could remember seeing her, even after her near-death at the mouth of Willow's *sine kot diabl.*

"Well, aren't you—most of you, anyway—just the pessimistic bunch," she snapped. "When was the last time any of you tried to do anything other than beat something into submission? You guys should have a little more faith in my skills. I *am* a demon, you know. At more than a thousand years old, I've seen and tried a few things you limited-life-span humans don't even know exist."

"And that would include spells," Xander said.

"Well, *duh!*"

"*Regeneration* spells?"

The second part of Xander's question was met with icy silence, but it didn't last long.

"I'm all for it," Giles said.

"There's a first time for everything," Dawn said.

"Yeah." Buffy grinned good-naturedly at her sister. "And we'll call you Cliché Girl for the rest of the day."

Dawn folded her arms. "Whatever. Every spell had to have a very first time that it was ever tried."

"And then forty-three times to get it right after that," Xander added. "But let's not talk about the mistakes."

"Exactly," Buffy said.

"I can wiggle my toes a little," Giles said.

Anya was the only one who heard that. "What else can you do?" she demanded. "Anything?"

"What mistakes?" Dawn demanded. "If it doesn't work, he stays the same as he is now. No biggie."

"Maybe," Buffy said. "But disappointment is a terrible thing to deal with, especially over something like this."

"I can stand. But it's really only a feat of balance more than anything else."

"Excellent!" Anya exclaimed.

"So what does that mean?" Dawn glared at Buffy. "We don't try at all? How do you know it'll fail if you don't even try? For crying out loud, I've heard you say that enough times."

"Okay," Anya said. "This is what we need. The moon is in Scorpio, which is the perfect phase for transformations. Whenever the rest of you stop arguing, you'll realize that's exactly what we're trying to achieve here."

Buffy shook her head. "That's not it at all. I just think that the risks outweigh the gain. If we can just wait a little longer—"

"Buffy, it's not your decision." Although even and not very loud, Giles's voice cut through all the babble in the room. "It's mine. And I want to do it."

Buffy opened her mouth to protest, then closed it. Of course he did. If it was her stranded in that wheelchair, wouldn't she? In fact, wouldn't she be willing to try just about *anything* to walk again? There was so much information in this shop, in the books, both good and bad, that filled the shelves, that it was probably a miracle he hadn't been tempted to try to concoct something on his own. "Well, I guess I'm outvoted," she finally said. "What do we do?"

Xander scrubbed at his eyes. "Are you sure this is a good idea, Giles? I mean, look at our history. Stuff has a way of seriously Murphy's-lawing in Sunnydale. Sometimes we don't even *know* it does." No one said anything, but they all knew he was talking about Willow's spell to bring Buffy back from the dead, and how they'd thought it had failed . . . unknowingly leaving a very much alive and—as a result of being yanked out of heaven and thrown back into her body—nearly insane Buffy buried alive in her coffin.

"It's a regeneration spell only in the vaguest sense of the word," Anya told them. "Giles isn't going to grow a new set of legs or anything like that."

"Good thing," Xander said. "Otherwise his pants won't fit."

Anya glared at him. "For those among us who only understand about fixing things with a hammer, what's regenerating—hopefully—is the damaged nerves in Giles's spinal column. I'm not all medically infused, so I don't know the technical mumbo jumbo for what's what. The down and nervy of it is that if he can *feel* his legs, he ought to be able to move them."

Dawn abruptly looked unhappy. "Okay, why does this suddenly sound really scary to me?"

Buffy took a deep breath. "I think it's the 'with feeling' part." She glanced at Giles but he didn't seem to be following her train of thought. "Anya, what if all Giles feels after the spell is . . . pain?"

"There's really only a very small likelihood of that," Anya said, but she paled a little and suddenly sounded a lot less confident.

"I'm willing to take that chance," Giles said. "I'd rather feel *something* than nothing at all. As Anya pointed out, if I can feel my legs, I ought to be able to move them."

"And possibly spend the rest of your life heavily sedated," Xander said darkly. "A friend of my dad's once went through a serious sciatica nerve problem. For about a week he didn't do much besides writhe on his bed." He shook his head. "It was a horrible thing to see. I can't imagine actually trading places with the man."

"If it comes to that, we can take him to the hospital and they can cut the nerves in his back or something," Anya suggested.

"Anya!" Dawn looked horrified.

"I'm just saying."

"Again," Giles said stiffly, "I'm willing to accept the risk." He pushed the wheelchair away from the table and turned it so that he was facing Anya. "When do we start?"

Anya's smile was a little forced at the edges, but she still drew herself up tall. "Today," she said. "One hour from now."

Since Xander had rebuilt the Magic Box, it had taken on a sort of medieval hunting lodge look—lots of rough-hewn wooden beams, exposed wood, and a few areas of brick and stonework where he'd not only patched smashed walls but decided to make them stronger. With the lights dimmed to almost nothing and the place illuminated by only a few strategically placed candles, it felt ancient, too—the atmosphere and what they were about to attempt combining to create a sort of pseudoslip backward in time. To Anya, it felt almost comfortable—she'd been in rooms just like this many times over the past centuries, and really, all they needed was a few period costumes, and maybe an oversized stone hearth and a roaring fire, to complete the picture.

The spell was her own creation and she'd set up her altar carefully. She'd been secretly working on this for a good two weeks before presenting the idea, never telling anyone about what was going on in her head. Everything she placed on the table had been researched, from the hows and whys of using it to the wheres of placement in relation to the items around it. The only not-so-perfect part was that it was incredibly complicated.

"You go here," she told Giles. "Facing the table. Buffy and Dawn, you guys move one on each side of him. Hold these." She handed Buffy a red candle signifying strength, and Dawn a green candle that represented healing. "Xander, you stand behind him and hold this black candle."

"Why do I get the black one?" he complained. "That doesn't seem so good."

"All these years in Sunnydale and you've learned zilch," she said. "Black is one of the most important colors," she said. "It will repel negative energy, plus it could have been a substitute for any other color that we don't have. Giles, you take this." Giles had obediently positioned his wheelchair and now reached for the gold candle she offered. "It signifies power of the male. Ordinarily I would never give a man such a thing, but tonight you're going to need all the power we can get into you."

Giles only nodded. He had too much going on in his head right now to question Anya's method or the ingredients of the coming enchantment. Frankly, all he could think about was the chance that he might walk again, might actually be on his feet in . . . what? A half hour? Yes, in a half hour, he might be able to stand up and walk away from this wretched wheelchair forever. The possibility was enough to take his breath away, fog his thinking, make him nearly incapable of following Anya's directions. He felt like he'd been confined to this metal monstrosity for years, watching the world go by, seeing Buffy and the others struggle along with him helpless to assist, yet it had hardly been a month or so. How did those people who found themselves limited in the same manner for years on end, for entire lifetimes, bear it? How did they wake each day and find the will to go on, to make the best of a truly horrific situation? Giles had always thought he was a strong man, a stronger Watcher, but this . . . this was simply too much for him to endure.

And if Anya failed . . .

No, he would not think like that, he would not even contemplate it. She would not fail, because she *must* not. He would go insane, he would—

No, he wouldn't.

He would endure, because he would have no choice.

Watching Anya and the others, their faces set in concentration, Giles realized that if the spell did not work, it was for their sake, not his, that he would, as that ludicrous old saying went, grin and bear it.

But oh, if it *did* work . . .

"Okay." Anya sounded a little breathless, the stress showing in her voice. "I'm going to lay out the altar first, and then I'm going to draw the circle around us all using cedar chips."

Xander's eyes widened. "Say, this doesn't involve fire, does it? As in smoking wood?"

"They use cedar in closets to keep the moths away," Dawn commented. "Is that what it's for here, to keep . . . whatever away?"

Anya shook her head as she began arranging things on a red velvet tablecloth she'd spread over the table. "No, it's for healing. Almost everything I'm using is for healing." They watched, fascinated despite their nervousness, while she set out a small brass chalice full of sliced apples, then sprinkled them with white carnation petals. Then she began to fashion an *Ansuz*, the rune that stood for healing, in the center of the cloth. One item after another started to form first the lefthand bar, then the two downward slanting bars that made it look like an angled *F* made of powdered cinnamon, garlic, marjoram, rosemary, thyme, ivy, and mistletoe. At the top end of the figurine Anya carefully placed a small moss agate, a milky-colored stone with a faint tint of green inside it, and at the ends of both side bars she fixed a tangerine-colored sunstone. Finally she ended the longest bar with a bloodstone. "This," she told them solemnly, "is to protect myself. There have been stories, rumors really, about these spells turning around on the witch who made them." She didn't elaborate, but they all knew what she was talking about.

"There," she finally said. She took a deep breath. "I think we're ready to light the candles and begin."

They all looked at one another, but no one could think of anything to say. "Excellent," Giles finally said in a low voice. "Then let's get started. What shall I do?"

Anya hesitated. "Just . . . sit there. And be ready to get healed."

Her voice was shaking slightly, and Giles knew,

suddenly, that it was her fear of disappointing him that was sapping her of confidence, pouring fear into the room's atmosphere. "It'll work, Anya," he said. He made his voice smooth and steady, willing everything he had into sounding as though he totally believed in her. "You'll do fine."

She stared at him for a moment, her eyes looking bright and liquid in the light of the candles already placed around the shop. Then she nodded, squared her shoulders, and started the ritual.

Walking slowly counterclockwise, Anya lit the candles that Buffy, Xander, and Dawn were holding, then finished her circle by lighting Giles's gold one. While she may have seemed unsure a few moments ago, now she called out in a strong, clear voice, over and over:

"Grannus and Nuada, ancient keepers of the healing powers, I ask you to come to us this night and bestow your favor upon Rupert Giles."

By the time she'd lit Giles's candle, she'd completed her opening invocation three times. They waited expectantly, but nothing seemed to be happening—

A small, warm draft ruffled the candle flames and the fine hairs on the back of each of their necks.

Xander swallowed as Dawn shuddered and started to turn to look behind her. "Be still," Anya said sharply. "Don't break the tone. You must stay put and not make a sound, no matter what happens." Dawn froze, then turned her gaze back toward Anya and the altar.

Frowning with concentration, Anya walked around to the back of the table to where she could face Giles across its expanse, careful to stay within the circle of cedar chips. From the tabletop, she picked up a sparkling white cord that they hadn't seen her place among the other items. She held it high, and her words flowed sweetly on the warm breeze; as she completed each sentence, her slender fingers worked a knot in the cord to go with it.

"Hear me, Grannus and Nuada! My knot of one, repair his bones. My knot of two, your powers use. My knot of three, make it be. My knot of four, be still no more. My knot of five, his nerve's revive. My knot of six, his spine is fixed. My knot of seven, the healing's given. My knot of eight, be changed, his fate."

The breeze had built to a full wind now, warm but not uncomfortably so, and while the candlelight flickered wildly, none of the flames went out. Finally Anya added her final statement:

"My knot of nine, it's healing time!"

What had been a wind suddenly built to gale force. The candles went out at the same time they all heard a low roar. Then, just as suddenly, the sound faded and they were all left waiting in the dark.

Giles felt perspiration slide down the side of his face. Surrounded by utter silence, he knew that the others were waiting for him, for some sign of, they hoped, success. He bit his bottom lip, then gathered all his concentration to try to move his legs.

And knew immediately that Anya's spell . . .

. . . had failed.

Chapter Eleven

"**W**hat?" Willow demanded. "I've never made any secret of what I gathered all of you together for. Why are we having this conversation *again*?" She threw up her hands. "God, I feel like I'm listening to the same song stuck on repeat on the stereo. Can't you guys just give it a rest?"

"How can you be so cavalier about something this important?" Njeri demanded. "We wouldn't keep bringing it up if we weren't so worried about it." She looked at the other women seated here and there around the loft and got nods of agreement. "If we didn't feel that we aren't *safe*."

"I am not 'cavalier'!" Willow threw up her hands. "I made you a golem, for crying out loud. There is no safer place in Sunnydale than where you are right now!"

"Exactly." Ena's calmer voice rose from the rear corner of the room, where she'd settled onto one of the full-sized floor pillows. "But we certainly can't stay here all the time, now can we? Not twenty-four/seven." She glanced around. "While you've decorated quite attractively, it's just not set up to be the Hellmouth's version of the Ritz Carlton." There were a few half-hearted chuckles. "You've barely room to keep poor Flo comfortable, and that's only because of her perpetual sleep."

"Yeah," agreed Ellen. "Come on, Willow. As employers go, you need to up the benefits."

Willow's mouth worked, but before she could think of anything to say, Anan had her own comments to throw into the criticism pot. "Offense would be nice," she said in a biting tone. "As a general would do in any good war. The two sides don't just stay in a no-win situation, you know. One always takes the offensive."

Willow shot the blond-haired witch an annoyed look. "This isn't a *war*. I don't have anything to fight over—"

"What about our *safety*?" demanded Njeri again. "Why isn't that worthy enough for you?"

"But you *are* safe. I just *told* you—"

"We're safe *here*, Willow," Ena said. "But what happens when we leave here? The former Watcher and the Slayer are quite powerful, and they have that vengeance demon convinced, at least for now, that she should be on their side." She looked at Willow through half-closed lids. "What happens when your friends decide to pick us off, one by one?"

"They're not my friends anymore," Willow said hotly. "They—"

"Then why aren't you willing to do something about them?" Anan asked. "Why do you keep stalling?"

Willow stared at Anan, then ground her teeth together. "Fine," she said shortly. "You want offensive, that's what you'll get." Face flushed with anger, she clapped her hands three times. *"Come to me,"* she hissed as the last bit of the third sound faded away. No one said anything, and that was a good thing, a *safe* thing. At the moment, she was angry enough to lash out at anything, and while it might have given her some temporary satisfaction, she had enough common sense to know that punishment was the last thing these women needed right now. She could easily put the whammy on them, but that would only breed even more resentment, like a rat bite festering beneath a pretty pink bandage. No—she had been lazy in dealing with this internal problem, and the time had come to fix it once and for all.

But what would happen to Buffy, Giles, and the others when she sent the golem after them?

Willow couldn't let herself think about that. She was a different person now, the flipside to the reticent little bookworm who had once been at Buffy's and Giles's beck and call. The power she had stored within her was nearly inconceivable compared to the timid high school girl who'd once freaked out because the human version of Anyanka had used her to try and perform an amulet retrieval spell. Had Willow possessed the power back then that she had now, Anya would have had her amulet back a hundredfold.

She would not worry about Buffy or Giles, or any of the others. This was their fault, anyway. Had Giles not monkeyed around and tried to kill these women, they would have never so much as noticed his miserable, stationary existence. The librarian might not have been as mobile as prebattle-with-Willow, but he would have been a whole lot safer. But no—he had hurt them, frightened them, *angered* them, made them want to attack. And now he—and by association, Buffy and the rest of the Scooby gang—were going to have to deal with the witches' retaliation, with *Willow's* retaliation.

So sad.

Too bad.

But what would happen if Buffy defeated the Riley-golem? If she destroyed it?

No. Such a thing wasn't possible, it was beyond the realm of reality. Willow didn't even have to think about that.

The floor shuddered once, then vibrated again. From where she sat on a ruby-colored stuffed chair, Amy gave the other women a smug, dark grin. "Gather 'round, ladies. It's show time. Now we get to see the Willow you've all been clamoring for."

At the farthest end of the loft, the door banged open, bouncing sharply off the wall behind it. The Riley-golem trudged through the opening, heading with single-minded purpose to where Willow waited. Nothing fazed it, nothing broke its focus—not even when it passed just a bit too close to Oz and the werewolf snarled and raked his razored claws across the mud-surfaced hand so tantalizingly close. If it felt pain, the golem didn't acknowledge it; one heavy swat to the outstretched paw made the red-eyed Oz howl in pain and retreat to lick his bruises.

"That's right," Willow whispered with a pleased smile. "You just come to mama."

Studying the golem from her position near the back, Amy thought she would have felt more comfortable had the creature made some kind of noise—a grunt, snarl, gasp . . . anything to break its eerie, brooding silence. It was way too much like the golem was pondering something—its fate, or perhaps the orders it was about to receive from its creator. Whatever went on in that dirt-filled mind, Amy didn't think she wanted to know about it.

Supposedly this thing contained the spirit of Riley Finn. If that were true, what if it also contained something else . . . something such as *resentment*? Amy knew from experience how that could poison your mind, how it could make you hate. She'd gone through enough of it when she'd spent all that time in the form of a rat, and then it had doubled because of that one, elusive time that Willow had changed her back for only a few seconds . . . but hadn't noticed before losing her hold on the accidental spell.

Oh, she could resent all right.

But still, life was full of possibilities, and why let old grudges bog you down? She could live again now, and enjoy, and if someday an opportunity presented itself for a little payback—nothing serious, mind you, and certainly not on the Warren à la Filet level—she'd be ready. And meanwhile—

Amy was just going to sit back and watch the show.

Golem.

Such a clumsy word, Willow decided as she watched her creation plod steadily toward her. Fitting, perhaps, but awkward sounding and menial. All that power, nearly unstoppable, harnessed inside a body fashioned only for servitude. On the other hand, that could only be for the best. Without knowing the secrets that had been used to create a particular golem, its target would find the golem was virtually immune to destruction, at least by most of the common physical methods. You gave the creature a task, and it worked at doing what it was told until the job was finished. Period.

And she was about to send this one after Buffy.

As the Riley-golem crossed the last few feet, Willow felt a smidgen of doubt, a tickle at the back of her neck. She could see the Ghost of Tara flickering in and out of view, depending on where she chose to stand— too much light and her beloved's spirit tended to get saturated by it and wash away. If it was too dark, the Ghost of Tara acted like a sponge for the darkness, soaking up the shadows until again, she could barely be seen. It was only in a certain light that Tara's specter was best seen, a sort of soft and glowing medium candlelight.

Yes, there she was, over by the fireplace, running a see-through hand over the bristling fur on the back of Oz's neck, seemingly trying to comfort the werewolf after his miniature spat with the Riley-golem. Now that Willow knew where she was, the bigger question was, why hadn't the Ghost of Tara said anything? Willow had expected it, the same old argument about right and wrong, Buffy and friendship, old times' sake, yadda yadda yadda. But the spirit had still said nothing.

Had the Ghost of Tara finally given up on Willow? If so, Willow knew she should be glad. And yet . . . she tried to suppress it, but wasn't there that most secret and hidden part of her that wondered if the Ghost of Tara couldn't rescue her from the life she'd chosen? The one filled with darkness and spells and creatures called into existence solely for the destruction of those with whom she'd once shared her world?

Willow could never admit that, even to herself. To do so would mean she was willing to acknowledge defeat, that she would accept the Ghost of Tara's repeated statements that Willow would fail in her attempts to bring Tara back. And to do *that*, if she understood correctly, would mean releasing Tara in all forms . . . forever.

She would *not* fail. If it meant giving up that last, minuscule bit of herself that wished this were all happening to someone else, the part that wanted nothing better than to run and hide from all the pain and loss, then so be it.

Standing before her now, her creation awaited her whim.

"I have instructions for you," she told it in a clear,

loud voice. "You will obey them, and return to me once you have carried out my desires. You will *not* fail."

If it understood what she was saying, the golem made no indication of it. No sound, no movement— not even the simplest shake of its head. It just stood there and waited for her to finish.

Outwardly, Willow looked calm and cold, all business. But inside . . . her gaze flicked briefly to the Ghost of Tara, which was still over by Oz and the great fireplace next to which he was chained. Why hadn't she said anything? Was it because she knew the golem would fail? But that made no sense—that knowledge had always made the Ghost of Tara all the more prone to advise Willow against sending it.

But what if it were the opposite? If the golem *was* going to succeed and destroy Buffy and the rest of them, then why wasn't the Ghost of Tara trying to stop Willow from sending it?

Unanswerable questions—if the Ghost of Tara wasn't talking, then nothing would come from speculation. Better that she concentrate on what was here and in the right now of things.

The Riley golem.

He—it—was at least seven feet tall. She knew he had to be really heavy, but Willow couldn't have guessed his weight; the mud-base for his frame threw any logical estimate based on human proportions out the window. With him standing in front of her, she realized she hadn't really looked closely at him since his creation, just sent him on downstairs to handle any worries before they had a chance to become problems.

From ten, maybe even five feet away, the golem seemed like nothing more than a giant guy made of dried dirt. Up close, however, the resemblance to his spirit-sake was startling. While she hadn't thought her sculpting skills were all that capable, the life force inside the thing had made all the difference in the world. It was like looking at a dirty and vaguely dried-up version of the real Riley Finn. And who could miss those intense hazel eyes staring out of the golem's face . . . even if they were focused straight ahead, blank and void of reason or intelligence?

But for all the golem was lacking in those two things, it certainly made up for it in raw strength and a blind determination to obey.

Willow glanced again at the fireplace, but the Ghost of Tara had moved away from Oz and was now concealed somewhere within the gloomier crevices of the loft. Perhaps the spirit had tired of arguing with Willow, finally gotten the celestial memo that she wouldn't be able to change Willow's mind about this, or for that matter, anything else . . . such as the resurrection. It was more than past the time for the spirit to accept reality anyway.

As for her coven, tonight Willow would finally quiet the dissension among them and show them that her intentions were definitely on the side of deadly serious. Njeri would see in Willow's actions the means to being safe, as would the others. Hopefully even Anan would look upon it as a sort of resolution for herself, the vengeance on behalf of Flo that she was still crying out for in her heart.

"Listen to my words, and obey," she told the Riley golem. "Look here."

Willow cupped her hands in front of her and held them still. A moment later a gentle glow began to seep from between her fingers. She let the light build a bit more, then spread open her hands to reveal a glowing mini-effigy of the familiar Magic Box. She raised her hands until they were eye level with the golem and all the creature could focus on was the glowing model floating on her palms.

"You know this place."

It was a statement rather than a question, but the golem still gave a ponderous nod of agreement. "You will go to it, and you will destroy it. Level it to the ground until not a single piece of wood or brick is left over twelve inches high."

Another slow nod.

"And you will kill everyone within it."

The Riley golem didn't bother to agree a third time. Knowing nothing but blind obedience, it simply turned and headed out of the loft to perform its task.

Chapter Twelve

"Giles, she won't even talk to me. Come on—when was the last time you remember Anya not talking?" Xander twisted his hands together and paced the area in front of the table. His eyes were still purplish-black, but the swelling around his nose had gone down enough to allow him to talk normally. "I mean, I know she's disappointed—hell, we all are, especially you—but she can't just clam up like this. Not when underneath that human exterior is a vengeance demon. They never shut up. It makes people suspicious. It makes *me* suspicious. Nervous, too." He glanced at Giles for confirmation. "Am I right?"

Giles nodded, but it was at best a barely-there acknowledgment. Xander started to say something else, but Buffy cut him off. "Xander, be quiet."

His eyes widened as he turned to look at her. "What? Why?"

"Because you're making too much noise," Dawn said. "I know Anya's always saying guys are insensitive, but even you shouldn't need an instruction manual for tact right now."

He frowned and looked from Dawn to Buffy, then back at Giles. A flush crept up his cheeks. "Aw, hey. I'm sorry. You're right—not exactly the poster child for understanding, am I?" He went back over to Giles and gave the older man's shoulder what he hoped was a comforting squeeze. "We'll work it out, Giles. We'll find a way. You know Anya. She can be as stubborn as a zombie is hard to kill. She'll try again."

Try again? Giles looked up at Xander's earnest expression and couldn't contradict him, couldn't find the heart to tell the young man that the possibility of another failure was unthinkable. He'd thought himself prepared for this, for the possibility . . . no, the probability that Anya's home-sewn incantation would fall short of its mark.

And yet . . . he'd had such *hope*. In that most hidden part of his mind, he had hoped, and maybe even prayed. His brain had whispered of possible varying degrees of success, of things such as even if he didn't walk, he might feel *something*. There might be some movement beyond his perpetual, secret struggle to move his toes. And where there was feeling—even if it was pain—there was, of course, nerve regrowth, the regeneration of which Anya has so bullheadedly worked toward.

But failure? Abject, unequivocal *failure*?

Despite everything, Giles had been completely unprepared for that.

In spite of still being confined to this damnable metal monstrosity, he was supposed to be able to offer reassurance to Anya, a pat on the back for all her hard work and a gold star for effort and all that. But how on earth could he comfort Anya when right now he very nearly hated her?

Now that Xander had finally stopped his chatter, Buffy could sit back and watch, and think, and blame herself for the whole damned thing.

Studying her former Watcher without him knowing it—or if he did, Giles didn't say anything—she dared, just for a bit, to try to put herself into his shoes. It wasn't something she often let herself do about anyone; she was too far removed from so-called normal people, too outside the realm of their capabilities to, at least in her mind, accurately guess at their feelings. How could she? She was the Slayer, and that awesome-sounding title came with a few extra-awesome side effects, like superhuman strength, almost bottomless courage, the ability to heal at a rate unheard of in normal humandom. And that healing—that was the thing that had to frost Giles's cookies right about now, wasn't it? Because if *he* had that, he'd probably be up and striding around the Magic Box, demanding to know when they were all going to get off their chop-chops and put an end to this Wicked Willow business.

But Giles didn't have that power to heal himself. If

anyone had failed around here, it wasn't Anya. It was her. Big Bad Buffy the Vampire Slayer didn't step in and do her part to stop Willow from making mush out of the nerves in Giles's back.

What, Buffy wondered, were they going to do if Anya could never get Giles to walk again? It was an ugly, unwanted path, but try as she might, Buffy couldn't force her mind to veer off in another, more positive direction. Instead it went down an even darker path.

What if she couldn't defeat Willow? Couldn't stop her from amassing what seemed like all the power in the known universe? Couldn't even find out why Willow even wanted all that high voltage to begin with? How could she *ever* be worthy as a Slayer if she couldn't defeat one evil Wiccan? But if that evil Wiccan was Willow, and if defeating Willow meant killing her, did Buffy really want to? *Could* she?

Buffy couldn't answer any of those questions. In fact, they were too painful to truly contemplate.

Dawn had never actually believed that Rupert Giles would be a cripple for the rest of his life . . . until tonight.

She didn't know whom to blame for this, but God, she wanted to blame *someone*. Yet everywhere she looked, she found some sort of reason for the way people had acted, a cause and effect that had ultimately led up to Giles's extremely limited new mode of mobility. There was no justification and certainly no sense of *Oh, it's okay that it happened because he did this.* Obviously nothing could justify what had happened, and nothing could make it all right. But justification wasn't the same as cause and effect. It wasn't the same as looking at a situation and dissecting it, then finding to her own shocked self that you couldn't find one true person who was at fault.

Everyone had contributed to this, and yet everyone had done their part, somewhere along the line, to try to stop it.

Moving quietly, Dawn got up and made her way to the kitchen. She poured herself a glass of cold water from the refrigerator and thought about the way her legs had worked to bring her in here, the way the muscles moved with each other to carry her weight forward—flex, push, stretch, flex, push, stretch.

Finished with her water, Dawn carried her glass over to the sink and set it down; when she turned to leave she bumped her knee against the cabinet door. Her reward was a sort of dull thump against her kneecap; it didn't hurt, but it was *there*, sensation, and that was sure more than Giles could say for everything south of his waist. She tried to imagine what it would be like for her to be where he was, how even the smallest, most taken-for-granted things would suddenly become huge projects. Taking a shower, changing her clothes, going to the bathroom, even retrieving something off the top shelf anywhere. All those things she effortlessly accomplished on a daily basis had suddenly gone from everyday nothings to near impossibilities for him.

And for Giles to have to face them for years to come? Decades? She'd be the last to admit that at her age she really didn't have much perception about the passage of time. There were great chunks of her life that felt like molasses dripping down a frozen tree trunk at the height of winter. Waiting for Christmas when she'd been younger, waiting for summer vacation, waiting for the next exciting school event or the next glance from some cute guy in class. But if she thought it took a long time for spring break to come around—

What the heck did Giles feel like, waiting to be able to walk again?

Especially now that he was faced with the reality that it simply might never come to be?

Next to having Xander leave her at the altar, Anya's failure at Giles's regeneration spell had to be the most disappointing thing in her life. Well, having her amulet smashed that first time had been pretty devastating, but since eventually she'd gotten her demonness back, that was out of the best-of running.

All kidding aside, she'd thought she was better than that. For crying out loud, she'd spent over a thousand years doing magick, and while it hadn't been anywhere near the level that Willow had ultimately grown into, Anya had been pretty adept at the small range presto-chango. She did a *lot* of research on that darned spell for Giles, covered every aspect she could think of, even digging around and finding gods of healing who were a little more obscure, just to be sure that they weren't inundated with requests. She'd covered the elements, made offerings to please the senses with the herbs, and written the request in the shape of an ancient rune in case they were only listening with half a godlike ear. She had the right color candles to strengthen and protect, the right circle. She'd had cedar chips and stones to represent the earth, she'd had fire, and she'd had—

No water. No blood.

The double realization made her sit upright. How could she have been so dense?

Just as quickly as Anya had straightened, she forced herself to relax again, hoping none of the others had noticed. No water, no blood, and not just any water would do—it would have to be holy water, blessed not necessarily by a priest or a church, but by methods generally accepted in the Wiccan way. She was almost certain these were the missing ingredients and the reason for the enchantment's failure, but . . . she had to be sure, absolutely *positive* that it would work if she tried it again, before she told the others. As crushing as her failure had been to her and the others, she couldn't imagine what a second failure would do to Giles. To put him through that again and have it be for nothing was simply unthinkable.

No one was paying any attention to her, and Anya felt a guilty pang as she looked at them. Each looked mired in his or her own little pond of misery, and she had done that, albeit unwittingly, by missing some key ingredient or two in the regeneration spell. The place actually looked more like a library than the Magic Box, with all these people trying to hide themselves behind the cover of some dry tome—as if Xander and

Dawn were actually up for recreational reading about the history of golem creation through the ages. Even Buffy had a book in front of her, although she was the only one honest enough to not bother opening it. Giles had his books and his ever-present notepad, but the paper was blank, and his eyes were focused somewhere in space.

Maybe they wouldn't even trust her enough to try again; if they refused, Anya certainly couldn't force them. Then again, Giles would probably have another go—he wouldn't be able *not* to try again—and while Buffy, Xander, and Dawn might grumble about it, Anya knew that they'd do what he wanted. For her part, Anya had to be absolutely certain that—

Something huge and heavy thundered against the Magic Box's locked front door.

And when no one moved to answer it quickly enough, the door shattered into a thousand pieces and the worst kind of trouble came through on its own.

Chapter Thirteen

She had done what the members of her coven wanted, and now Willow decided it was time for them all to sit back and watch the fun.

While the other women waited, she went to a tall, antique cabinet and flung the heavy doors wide with as much flair as she could pull off without seeming really hokey. The door hinges of the chest, which had to be at least two hundred years old, gave a satisfying creak, a sound that was part old haunted house and part fingernails on blackboard. A great combination, one designed to make a person both shudder and clench their teeth at the same time.

Made of pitted and scarred black walnut and showing half a hundred different macabre carvings beneath a heavy coating of discolored varnish, no one but Willow was allowed in this cabinet and the doors would open only for her—even Giles's relocation spell hadn't been able to touch it. Inside were a couple of shelves now holding some of her more extra-special things, things that had previously been scattered around the loft and which had been the hardest to replace after the Giles-generated whirlwind had gone through. A few specific demon pieces, a couple of ancient artifacts, scrolls containing certain very important information that she was going to need to resurrect Tara, and, of course, her new crystal viewing ball.

She carried the ball and its stand to the table closest to the center of the room and set it up on the waiting royal green velvet tablecloth, then she motioned for the others to crowd around.

Willow gave them all a dark smile as she saw their anticipation building. "What fun," she asked, "is crashing a party if you can't see the chaos?"

On that, Willow reached out with her forefinger and tapped the top of the crystal globe. It came to life instantly, sending a hundred jagged lines jumping around inside it, all originating from where her finger touched its exterior. It looked like one of those lightning lamps the novelty stores sold at all the malls, except in another five seconds this one cleared up on the inside and turned into something else entirely.

A lot of Wiccans had so-called viewing balls, foggy-edged things whose centers hinted at movement that might or might not actually be happening—most of the time what was seen in the center was more a matter of interpretation. This one was a whole different glass animal; right now, it showed the very room

Willow and the women were in, every detail mirror-reflected in complete perfection except for the edges, where the ball's roundness distorted the image.

In a whisper so quiet that only those closest to her heard it, Willow told it, *"Magic Box."*

The ball's internal lightning storm returned instantly, this time etched in a thousand miniature scarlet bolts. It cleared as suddenly as it had begun, and then there it was, the inside of the Magic Box, so clear they might have been looking through a tiny window.

For a secret moment, one in which she hated herself for her own weakness, Willow felt a pang of nostalgia shoot through her even though the interior of the shop had been completely redesigned. It felt . . . weird, as though just for an instant she was falling away from some kind of hold, as though she had lost her grip on a rope in the darkness that might save her from some unnamed monster in the dark. Then the sensation was gone, and she was once again fully grounded in her loft and with her coven around her, and waiting to watch the destruction of the people who had become the most problematic things in the physical realm of her life.

The thing that burst through the door shouldn't have been a surprise. With the exception of Buffy, every one of them had seen it in the alley outside Willow's building, lumbering around like some kind of cartoon mud-pie man, except that it had a whole lot more punch.

But to take it inside, right *here* and into the safety of the Magic Box, that took the situation to a whole new level of terror.

There was no time for nonsense like freezing in place or being paralyzed for a couple of seconds while they mentally assessed the threat coming at them. The crash of the golem's entrance sent them leaping in every direction to avoid the flying pieces of wood. Giles inexpertly spun his wheelchair out from under the table and began rolling it in reverse, although he figured he was already in trouble; he couldn't fight, he couldn't run, and the golem was damned near unstoppable.

Xander deserved the credit for making the first move to try to fight the thing. He snatched up one of the heavy library chairs they used around the table and rushed it, straining with the effort of holding up the chair like a battering ram. The golem swatted the chair aside like it was brushing away an annoying gnat; the chair flew out of Xander's hands, splintering when it hit the floor a good ten feet away. For a microsecond, Xander stared stupidly at where the chair had been in his hands, then the golem swung its fist at his face. Still oversensitive about the damage already done, Xander dropped to the floor and went under the punch, grateful that Mr. Mud here wasn't well-equipped in the high-speed department.

"A little help here!" he yelled, and rolled out of reach as the golem leaned over to grab him.

As Dawn scrambled out of the way, Anya leaped between the golem and Giles, then hauled the heavy table in front of her. It wouldn't stop the walking pile of mud, but it might slow him down, give Giles a chance to roll himself out the back door. A grand idea, but the dirt-monster plowed forward and the table might as well have not even been there. Figuring she'd have a better chance of standing up to the coming blow, Anya morphed into demon mode just as the golem pulled back to strike.

The attack never came. Buffy leaped onto the golem's back, wrapped her left arm around the creature's throat, and hung on for all she was worth. Mr. Mud forgot about Anya—thankfully—and did an awkward spin as it tried to throw Buffy off. When that didn't work, it tried a lumbering half-jump, a move that was almost embarrassing to watch given the golem's considerable weight. By the time it was through with its second hop, Buffy had raised a small hand ax—now Anya knew Buffy had dashed to the weapons closet in those first few moments of the golem's visit—and was energetically hacking away at the back of its head. Little chunks of hard-packed dirt were sailing in every direction by the time the golem's earthy bit of a brain told it there were bigger things to worry about than the human being on its back.

Oddly, the creature had not made a sound the entire time, and even having its scalp disappear in mini-chunks wasn't enough to make it vocal. It turned clumsily again, then began to back toward the nearest wall.

Dawn's head popped up from where she'd hidden herself behind the counter. "Buffy, the wall!" she cried. "Get off it before—"

Too late.

Buffy wasn't sure how much this walking pile of glued-together dust weighed, but it was *a lot*. When she got sandwiched between its back and wall—wouldn't you know it was the new brick part that Xander had put in—all the air was squashed out of her lungs, and those were definitely stars and little twittering birds whirling around in front of her eyes. All thoughts of hanging on went out of her head, as did any notion of hack-'em-up; she dropped to the floor.

Xander scrambled to his feet and grabbed one of the smashed chair legs, yelping as he got a nasty dose of splinters in his palm, then charged the golem. It ignored him and turned slowly to face Buffy, towering over her like a giant about to step on a bug. Xander rushed forward and brought the chair leg down on its back once, then twice, but it paid no attention as it leaned down and—

Stopped.

Xander beat on it a few more times, then paused in confusion. Still holding the chair leg—or what was left of it, anyway—aloft, he looked from the golem to Giles, then back again. Finally he lowered the chair leg and slowly inched around to the side of the mud-man. "Uh . . . hello?" He waved a hand experimentally in front of the creature's face, but its hazel eyes never blinked. "I'm a little afraid to ask, but . . . anyone in there?"

Dawn came cautiously out from behind the counter and made a wide path around the golem's other side, until she could crouch next to Buffy. "Buffy, are you all right?" She glanced nervously up at the golem, but it still hadn't moved or changed the direction of its intense gaze. "Come on, Buffy. We need to get you up and outta here before Mr. Mud Pie recharges his Duracells."

Buffy groaned and sucked air into her bruised lungs. The inhalation started an ache that went all the way through her chest and ribs to the muscles in her back. "Now I know what the guy at the bottom of those football pile-ups feels like," she mumbled. She waved her hand in the air until Dawn grabbed it. "Help me get up."

Xander grabbed one elbow and Dawn got the other. When Buffy was upright and steady, she regarded the golem suspiciously, but it didn't seem inclined to move. Finally, still keeping her distance, she asked, "Do you think it's still alive?"

On the other side of the room, Giles motioned impatiently at Anya to get him around the debris and over to where the others stood. "Let me see." When enough of the broken furniture had been moved aside so Giles could get close, he craned his neck to study the creature. "Fascinating," he said. He rolled his wheelchair back a few inches, even though the golem still hadn't moved. "But without knowing specifically why it stopped attacking, I'd say it's still quite dangerous. For all we know, Willow could have some kind of telepathic link to it and she could be controlling it from afar."

"Then why did she stop?" Xander said. "Why not just finish the job?"

Giles shook his head. "Perhaps she had an attack

of conscience, or she simply got sidetracked by something else. In any case, my suggestion would be to clear out of here before this creature comes back to whatever it has that passes for awareness."

"Great idea," Dawn said heartily. "Come on, Buffy. Let's go."

"Wait a second." Buffy sounded a little wheezy, but she was already nearly recovered. She stared up at the golem intently, tilting her head to one side in concentration. They all stared at her as she stared at the golem, then—

"Riley?"

The golem blinked.

"Buffy," Giles said nervously, "be careful. You don't know that for certain."

But she wasn't listening, and now she was standing only a few inches away from it. If the golem wanted to, it had only to enfold her in its massive arms and crush her in a golem-hug.

She took a step closer anyway. "Is that you, Riley? Are you . . . in there?"

The golem blinked again and shifted its gaze from the top of Buffy's head to her eyes.

"Oh my God," she said softly. "You *are* in there."

And they all stood and stared at the golem for a long, long time.

Chapter Fourteen

For a shocked second, no one said anything at all.

Then Amy broke the uncomfortable silence. "Well," she said in disgust as she sat back, "that was certainly less than successful. Have you got any more tactical ideas?"

Standing there, Willow hid her hands in the folds of her robe. They were bunched into fists, and she was so angry at this turn of events that they were *itching* to do something—anything—to *anyone* who got on her bad side. And right now, her bad side was pretty much in all four directions. "That was certainly . . . unexpected," she finally said in a low voice.

"Tell us something we *don't* know," Njeri said sarcastically, "like how if you're so high and all-powerful, you didn't know this could happen."

Willow started to glare at her, but Ena stood brusquely, ruffling her skirt and making as much of a fuss about her velvet dress as possible so she could pull Willow's attention away from Njeri's patently dangerous surliness. "Let's not bicker," she said. "It certainly won't change the outcome of this unfortunate incident."

Turning her back to the table, Willow raised a hand to her forehead. "I don't understand," she said, half to herself, half to the others. "The insertion of a vengeful or spurned spirit is supposed to make the golem stronger. It shouldn't have made it just freeze up."

"I don't think he's paralyzed," said Cybele. She was leaning forward and peering into the viewing crystal, her brown eyes narrowed in concentration. "Look."

Willow turned back to the ball as the others crowded back around. Cybele was right; the golem *was* moving again. For a drawn-out and hopeful moment Willow was sure that the battle was going to start anew. Maybe the golem had run out of energy or something, or been temporarily frozen by some phrase that pesky librarian had remembered at the last moment. The crystal viewing ball sadly lacked the ability to generate sound effects, but it wasn't such a far-fetched idea and it fit what they could see of the action. Surely the next step would be witnessing the life crushed out of Buffy and her cohorts.

But . . . no.

With a cry of rage, Willow picked up the crystal view ball and hurled it against the farthest wall, where it burst into thousands of shimmering pieces.

"Do you think he understands us?" Dawn peered at the golem, but she looked ready to jump for the ceiling if it moved again.

Buffy didn't have an answer for that, only a dozen or more new questions that ran along the same vein. The golem *had* proved to them that it was still an animated entity; apparently it had the unnerving desire to lumber after Buffy wherever she went. Since she couldn't get it to *not* do that, she'd finally just sat on one of the library chairs and waited to see what would happen. Now the golem was just standing there next to her, like some sort of statue that could come to life at any moment. Only its eyes seemed alive, and when she looked into them, Buffy knew without a doubt that Riley's spirit was trapped in there. Was he miserable? Did he have sentience and *know* what he was, and where he was, yet be unable to control his own existence and destiny?

God, that was way too much like Giles being trapped in the wheelchair.

Xander cleared his throat and looked at the golem nervously. "I just hope he doesn't change his mind about staying in good-guy mode," he said as he gathered up pieces of the shattered chair. The table had fared better, although every week that went by seemed to put more "character" into it. Xander tossed the load of wood pieces into a pile by the front entrance, then eyed the remains of the door unhappily. He'd have to board that up overnight just to keep out the general riff-raff. Without realizing it, he gingerly touched the bridge of his nose. "I don't think we could hold up to much more of his bad-guy side."

Giles nodded thoughtfully. "Very true. Right now he seems almost docile, but how do we know that this is a permanent state of behavior? It could be a ploy to get us to lower our defenses."

Buffy shook her head. "I don't think it is. I mean, look at it—at *him*. Riley's in there somewhere. I just know it. Maybe he can't do anything about it, like talk or think, but he has enough will to know he doesn't want to hurt us."

"Check that," Anya said. She was fiddling around behind the counter, doing something that the others couldn't see. "Your big and muddy pet didn't have any problem putting the hammer down on us. Twice, remember? It just doesn't want to put any sore spots on *you*."

"I agree," Giles said. "It's obvious that Riley's spirit recognizes you and is resisting whatever orders Willow gave it."

"Oh, I think we know what Miss High and Wiccan wanted it to do," Anya said darkly. "Just look at him. He's like some kind of giant-sized voodoo doll."

Giles pressed his lips together. "Perhaps. In the meantime, I think it's very important that we devote ourselves to doing whatever we can to stop the golem from doing any further damage to us or anyone else."

Buffy looked at him knowingly. "And this also means?"

Giles nodded again. "I suppose it means freeing Riley to return to . . . wherever he was originally in his afterlife."

"That's great," Anya said from behind him. "But first let's get you mobile."

Giles shot her a haunted glance. "I appreciate your efforts, Anya. But we can't sit around waiting for me to get some nerve endings back into my legs. Even if this comes to pass, it might take months for the muscles to—"

"Let's try again."

Dead silence.

Anya swallowed nervously. She felt about an inch tall under the four pairs of eyes locked onto her. "Look," she said, "no one, well, except Giles, of course, knows how disappointing it was to me to have that spell fail. But I know where it went wrong, I know what got left out. And I'm telling you, it *will* work if we try it again." She paused, and when no one said anything, she repeated herself as much to try to reach them as to make herself believe it. "It *will*."

As far as Giles could tell, Anya was using nearly the same setup. There were a few things placed on the red velvet tablecloth that he couldn't quite see because of the way larger objects blocked his view. He thought he saw her carefully position a small silver knife he'd never seen before, but he couldn't be sure. Why would she need a knife for a healing ritual? He was burning with reluctant curiosity, but he forced himself to stay quiet, not ask questions, not break Anya's concentration. He hadn't allowed himself to research this, to hunt for a spell that might heal his legs; he'd been too wary of the disappointment, of the frustration of not finding it right away, of the fear of not finding it at all. So when Anya had come up with this idea the first time, he had been terrified but elated. Now, after her first failure, he was just terrified.

"So," Anya said, when she'd carefully positioned

them in a repeat performance pattern, "there are a few things we have to do differently this time." She glanced at each of them in turn, but they only waited for her instruction. She was vaguely glad that no one seemed in the mood to argue or question; she wasn't sure she could have kept up her determination if they'd protested. She was still half-inclined to abandon the effort, but every time she got too close to doing just that, she would feel, literally *feel*, her own legs. Then she would think about Giles and the way that feeling had been denied him, how he might never have those feelings again.

So the show would go on.

"The ritual is almost the same," Anya said. "One of the mistakes I made was that Nuada requires silver, and I used a brass chalice. I've fixed that."

Buffy blinked at her, but was careful not to move from where Anya had positioned her to Giles's right. "That was it? Brass instead of silver made it not work?"

"It wasn't just that," Anya answered. "My rope is a lot longer—nine feet instead of inches. I have two chalices now. One with the offering of apples and rose petals, and another holding specially blessed holy water. We'll also have two of the symbols for healing, the *Ansuz*. One will be made on the altar, just like the last time." She licked her lips. "The other has to be cut into Giles's forehead to mark him as the undisputed recipient of the healing. The holy water in the second silver chalice is to purify the silver knife."

For a long moment, as Anya and the others

focused on Giles and waited for his reaction, only the sound of their breathing could be heard in the room. It was hard for Anya to see the librarian's face in the darkness, impossible to know what he was thinking or how he felt about the physical part of it.

"All right." Giles's quiet answer broke the astonished silence.

"Oh, no," Buffy said. "Absolutely no way."

"Anya, you can't *cut* him!" Dawn cried. "For God's sake, he's not a roast!"

"What if it doesn't work again?" Buffy demanded. "He'll be stuck with this huge scar on his forehead. If that happens, will you be able to fix it? Make it go away?"

"Buffy's right, Anya." Xander's face looked pinched and unhappy. "Without a guarantee, you just can't do this."

"And okay, has anyone besides me noticed the way-too-much like human sacrifice aspect?" Dawn asked.

Anya just stood there, taking in all the comments but not saying a word, watching as they abandoned their assigned spaces and crowded around Giles in a nearly protective circle. *Funny,* she thought sourly, *how I could go from good guy to bad guy in the space of five seconds.*

"Would you all please go back to where Anya placed you?" Giles didn't raise his voice, but the words managed to break through all the babble anyway.

"Giles, you're not actually going to do this, are you?" Buffy stared at him incredulously. "This isn't face-painting at the carnival that Anya's suggesting."

"It should heal when his legs do," Anya offered.

"'Should' being the focus word here," Dawn pointed out in a sharp voice.

"I will take my chances." Giles's voice was louder this time, much more no-nonsense. "I do believe that ultimately this is *my* choice, and while I appreciate everyone's concern, may I remind you that a chance never taken is a possible opportunity forever missed." Gathered around him, their candles now bathed his head in flickering light and shadow. He turned his face back toward Anya. "I don't believe Anya can wait to perform this enchantment another time. I recall from the first attempt that there are celestial alignments to be factored in, and who knows what else. I've no doubt Anya put a lot of work and research into this that we don't even know about." He closed his eyes briefly, then opened them; they were clear and without doubt. "I truly believe it's now or never."

Buffy started to argue more but Giles held up his hand, effectively putting an end to the discussion. "No more," he insisted. "Now, if you're going to be a part of this, go back to where Anya told you to be."

With their faces creased with worry, Buffy and the others slowly returned to their stations, then stood there as Anya began the ritual with the making of the familiar circle of cedar chips. She'd already arranged her new altar with much the same accouterments as before, with the exception of the silver chalices and the small, sharp knife. The smell of the sliced apples and carnation petals mingled pleasantly with the scented candles as she stepped up to each of them and touched a long wooden match to each candlewick.

Next Anya carefully constructed her first *Ansuz* the same way she had before, out of the powdered spices and herbs, the ivy, and the mistletoe. These scents, combined with the apples and the warm candles, drifted on the air around them, reminiscent of long-lost holidays, when hot, home-baked pies cooled on the counter and spiced cinnamon cider simmered on the stove. If only what they were involved in here were that easy, that comforting.

Finishing off her table rune with the same stones as she had before, Anya inhaled slowly, willing herself to have the courage to do what was next. She picked up the knife gingerly, as though she were afraid it would turn itself around and sink into her own unresisting flesh. When she was sure of her grip on it, she carefully dipped its tip into the holy water in the silver chalice, turning it so that the moisture coated both sides and ran all the way down the blade. Next to the knife was a white silk cloth that Giles hadn't noticed before; Anya dipped it in the holy water, then gently wiped it across his forehead. She folded it neatly and put it aside, then returned to where she could stand directly in front of him. When the incantation came out of her mouth, the words were slightly revised and her voice was again strong and clear, utterly determined, as she lifted the blade high above her head.

"Grannus of the minerals, and Nuada of the silver hand, ancient keepers of the healing powers, I ask you to come to us this night and bestow your favor upon Rupert Giles."

Before Giles could think about it further, Anya leaned down and drew a straight, stinging line down the center of his forehead.

He stifled a gasp and circled his free hand around the arm of his wheelchair, gripping as hard as he could to stop himself from automatically reaching for his face, praying he wouldn't lose his grip on his gold candle.

"Gannus of the minerals, and Nuada of the silver hand," Anya began again. Blood was already dripping down the bridge of his nose and following the contours of his nostrils as she finished the second repetition, then drew the top downward bar of the rune. Just as painful, but at least the cut wasn't quite as long. He was having to squeeze his eyes shut now to keep the blood out of them, and in the background he thought he heard Dawn whimper as Anya began her final recitation and the blade carved the bottom bar. Again, it was painful, but Giles had certainly endured far worse in his lifetime.

And this time, when the breeze came, it was a hell of a lot stronger.

The candles barely managed to stay lit, and Giles thought that was probably because Anya had charmed them ahead of time. She put the bloody knife down on the wet cloth she'd used to prepare Giles's forehead, then picked up what she had substituted for her previous piece of cord, a thick white rope. This time, instead of holding it up, she snaked one end of it around Giles's right knee and began winding it upward, working heavy knots into it at even, one-foot intervals as she spoke, wrapping it around his legs, his arms, his shoulders, his neck. Her incantation was nearly identical to the first time.

"Hear me, Grannus and Nuada, keepers of the precious healing powers! My knot of one, repair his bones. My knot of two, your powers use. My knot of three, make it be. My knot of four, be still no more. My knot of five, his nerve's revive. My knot of six, his spine is fixed. My knot of seven, the healing's given. My knot of eight, be changed, his fate."

And at last, in the midst of a nearly storm-force wind, Anya shouted her final words and yanked the last of the cord into a tight knot.

"My knot of nine, it's healing time!"

The wind went suddenly hot, uncomfortably so, and the candles winked out. Giles gasped as darkness overtook the room. Everything was so black, unnaturally so, and for an overlong, frightening moment, he could have sworn that there was someone else, some*thing* else, in the Magic Box with them—something bigger than they were, indefinable and unpredictable; something that was looming over him and judging his worth in eyes that had seen the measure of men a million times through the ages.

Would he be found worthy?

Or wanting?

Sitting there in the dark, Giles was suddenly completely sure that he was alone in this. Not just in the Magic Box, but in his life and what he would do with it right now, in this moment, and in what he had faced in the past and would deal with in the future. There was no one to help him, no one to do it for him. No matter what Anya's best efforts had been, no matter what Buffy and Xander and Dawn tried to do to help, he would ultimately have to do this himself.

Giles's slashed forehead throbbed and stinging perspiration mingled with the blood flowing freely down his face. His candle was gone, fallen aside, and now his hands were clenching the wheelchair's arms and his fingers spasmed as he forced them to let go. He strained and felt his toes wiggle, that same small and elusive movement that he had worked so hard to call his own since the night he'd awakened in the hospital bed and Dr. Berelli had given him the bad news.

The muscles in his arms strained as he hauled himself upright in the dark. An accomplishment? Not much—as he'd told the gang before, he had managed to stand on his own, and to balance there like one of those idiotic clowns on stilts. Doing it in the dark was doubly troublesome, because it instilled in him an odd sense of vertigo, forcing him to fight the sensation that at any second he was going to topple into an abyss.

"Giles?"

Anya's voice floated through the dark, sounding scared and faraway. "Are . . . are you there? Are you all right?"

"I'm right here, Anya." His voice was hoarse, like his throat was filled with sand. "I'm fine."

From somewhere in the blackness to his left rear came Xander's voice. "Are you, you know, cured?"

Still disoriented, Giles automatically tried to turn in the direction of Xander's voice. The attempt made him whack his knee painfully on the corner of the table, and he set his jaw against the expletive that almost escaped his lips. "Well, I can't rightly tell—"

Wait.

Somewhere in the inky area that was below his own body, Giles's knee throbbed, evidence of his encounter with the hard wooden corner. Elation surged through him, but Giles tried to force it away. Just because he could feel something didn't mean he was cured. It didn't mean he could *walk*. "I'm not sure," he amended.

"You're not sure?" Dawn repeated. She sounded like she was on the other side of the room. "How can—"

"Oh, for heaven's sake," Buffy said. "Xander, go turn on the light."

"Got it," he said. There was a crash, and an "Ommphf," and finally the overhead light snapped on.

Giles stared at all of them staring at him.

Okay, so he was upright, but then he knew that. And he knew about the pain in his knee, which told him without a doubt that sensation had returned. The interesting thing about the whole situation was not that he was standing, but that he was standing a full fifteen feet away from his wheelchair.

"Oh!" was all Anya said.

Giles looked down at his legs, and then at the floor. In the grand scheme of his life, he really hadn't been confined to a wheelchair for that long, but the ground had never looked so far away. The vertigo hit him again and he tilted forward; one hand reached for the table, but he was too far away. And when the forward motion continued, his right foot automatically, miraculously, slid out to steady his balance.

He was walking again.

Chapter Fifteen

"**H**ow could you do this?" Willow demanded. "How could you let me down like this?"

The Ghost of Tara stood in front of her, ethereal and impassive, silent. Willow waited for her to answer, and when she didn't, she pounded the table in frustration. "Talk to me, damn it! If you're going to be here, you might as well say *something*!"

Finally the Ghost of Tara seemed to focus on Willow. *"I don't know why you're so angry, Willow. You made it clear you didn't want to hear my advice, so this time I stayed out of your plans."*

"What are you talking about?" Willow demanded hotly. "I always listened to you!"

"No, you didn't. You never believed me before. Why would I have reason to think you'd believe me this time?"

Willow started to argue, then just threw up her

hands and stormed off. The members of her coven had gone home, but not until after their recriminations and unspoken accusations had made her feel about an inch tall. For God's sake, if she couldn't make her own creation obey her will, how was she going to make them obey her? And how could she actually resurrect her lover? Too many failures had left her with a serious self-confidence problem.

"You're very powerful, you know."

Willow jumped as the Ghost of Tara suddenly materialized in front of her. "W-what?"

"You're very powerful." Tara's spirit locked gazes with her, and Willow looked away after realizing she could see right through her form. She hated that, hated knowing what it meant. *"Some would say you're the most powerful Wiccan in the world right now."*

"Great," Willow said bitterly. "Throw me a party so we can all gather round and see where it's gotten me."

"My point exactly," the Ghost of Tara said. *"The accolades aren't exactly pouring in. Why don't you think about using all that power for good rather than evil?"*

Willow folded her arms and looked at the specter defiantly. "I'm not *that* evil. If I was, I'd be raining destruction down on Sunnydale just for the fun of it, you know."

The Ghost of Tara shrugged. *"Not without purpose—that isn't like you. In some ways, you* have *lost your purpose. In others, you've focused your energy on things that will not come to be. You'd be happier if you simply returned to your original life."*

"My original life?" Willow looked at the Ghost of Tara in astonishment. "Did you actually *think* about what you just said?" It was all she could do not to start sweeping things off the tabletop. "Or maybe because you're a ghost, you don't actually think, or maybe you just don't *feel*. I might have gained all these powers, but *you've* lost the ability to understand!"

"Not at all. I just know—"

"No, you don't!" Willow interrupted shrilly. "You don't know *anything*! What are you? Some kind of . . . cosmic *substance*, floating around in front of me and constantly telling me to stop doing this, or don't do that. You aren't even *real*!" She glared at the spirit. "You aren't even *Tara*!"

The Ghost of Tara looked at her sadly. *"Oh, Willow. I am Tara, but there's no way for me to make you understand the changes I've gone through. You say I don't understand you, but I do. I see it all—your thoughts, your heart, your pain. And while I don't always know everything, I can tell you right now that you'll never be able to bring me back. Things have gone too far."*

"You said yourself that you don't always know everything," Willow said stubbornly. "Do you know the mind of the universe? All the possible coulds and woulds and might-bes?" When the Ghost of Tara didn't answer, Willow raised her chin. "That's what I thought. You might be d-d—" She coughed, unable to bring herself to actually say the d-word to the spirit's face. "Gone," she finally put in. "You might be gone, but you can't see into the future. You just want me to think you can."

"I'm not gone, Willow. I'm right here."

"Oh, spare me the word dancing." Willow squeezed her eyes shut, then opened them again. The Ghost of Tara was still there, still staring at her with those nearly transparent eyes. "You're not really Tara, you know," she told the spirit in a low voice. "You're a . . . *part* of her, yes, but not the real thing. There are a thousand things different, a thousand things missing. This is why I can't fully accept you, why I hardly ever say your name." She swallowed, fighting the abrupt sting of tears at the corners of her eyes. "I can't accept you like this. I won't; it would be too much like surrender, like saying 'Okay, you really *are* dead.' I won't do that."

"There will come a time when you will have no choice."

Willow shook her head. "No, you don't really know that. Like I said, you don't really know *everything*. If you did, you'd show me how much you love me by telling me how to bring you back."

In some ways Giles felt it was the world's biggest miracle. All right—it was the world's biggest miracle to *him*, although the celebration that had taken place in the Magic Box after they'd all realized he could walk again made him feel like it extended to everyone else, too. There were things that had happened to them that overshadowed it by milestones (Willow's resurrection of Buffy came immediately to mind), but this was the here and now, and even that monumental event seemed to have been forgotten in the heat of his regained mobility.

It wasn't all tea and roses. He discovered right off the bat that he tired very quickly, and the fact that his muscle had already lost a good portion of their toning and left him weak aggravated him no end. That, Giles knew, would change, and if he was able to progress at the rate he wanted, it would change damned quickly. Right now he was lucky if he could walk the length of the Magic Box a couple of times before having to sit. Even so, as far as he could discern, there was nothing remaining that was actually *damaged* about his legs. They were simply disused and had to be reminded that it was necessary to carry him. His strength would come back soon enough.

"We should have a party," Anya announced. "To celebrate."

Dawn perked up. "Parties are fun. I could invite a few friends." At Buffy's look, she added, "Just kidding."

"A good thing," Xander commented, "because we'd really have a hard time explaining mud-face."

"Xander, stop it," Buffy said sharply. "What if Riley can hear you?"

But Xander just snorted. "Come on, Buffy. Look at him. If he could hear you, don't you think he'd actually be able to do stuff or something? Respond somehow to your questions?" He thought that even a grunt would be an improvement over the inhuman lump of dirt standing there and staring at them. No, it wasn't staring at them. It was staring at Buffy. The whole situation was unnerving.

"They say that someone in a coma can still hear what you say," Dawn said. "He could be like that—

able to hear but, like, frozen or something. Paralyzed."

Anya came around the counter and went up to the Riley-golem, examining it closely. It didn't move, didn't shift its field of vision from the beeline it had put on Buffy since it realized that she was there and apparently knew who she was; now it seemed content to stay in that one spot, and had done so since the big battle had ended and the gang had cleaned up this newest round of destruction. The thing didn't even blink when Anya waved her hand briskly in front of its bright hazel eyes. "Hello? Are you in there?" She stopped and stepped back. "I know Riley was into military minimal wordage, but this is ridiculous," she said finally. "What do you think, Giles? Do you think he can understand us?"

Giles looked up when he heard his name, then forced himself to concentrate. He'd been only half paying attention, but the time when he could focus on himself had ended. Things were back to normal—or they would be soon enough—and he needed to refocus on the golem and the problem of Willow. He'd been sitting, resting a bit, but now he rose, never once taking for granted the muscles that responded to his commands and the nerves that felt the floor through his shoes and allowed him to balance, and walked over to the golem.

"While I'd say without a doubt that the golem contains a part, if not all of Riley's spirit, I don't believe he truly understands," he finally decided. "We knew Riley well, and he knew us. Even without the presence of Buffy, he would have never attacked us. There is a big part of the essence that's controlling this creature that is functioning only on the most basic level—that of obeying orders."

"Then why did he stop?" Buffy asked.

Giles peered at the unblinking hazel eyes of the golem. "I believe that whatever there *is* of Riley inside of it essentially overpowered its own rudimentary commands. A battle of wills, I suppose. Limited, but nevertheless still there." No one said anything and Giles had a chance, slightly unwelcome, to think more about Riley and this creature. In a way, what Riley was enduring—or, God willing, he didn't know he was enduring—was very much like what Giles had gone through: being imprisoned by one's own body. He blinked, then continued. "As long as the Riley part continues to control it, we should be okay."

"Well, call me crazy," Dawn said. "But—"

"Okay, you're crazy," Xander obliged.

Dawn shot him an annoyed look, then continued. "Buffy, why don't you try telling it . . . *him* to do something simple, like sit or something."

"He's not a dog," Buffy said.

"Of course he's not," Giles agreed. "But Dawn does have a point. He has to at least be able to follow primary orders. How else would Willow have been able to send him over here?"

Buffy looked at Giles, then focused on her fingers, picking at the fingernails almost sullenly. "I can't believe she'd do that. I know that on the surface, Willow seems like she's evil. But I can't help but believe that underneath she's the same old person. I don't know why she's doing the things she's doing, but there's got to be a reason, something we don't know about."

"Well, hey," Anya said caustically. "Why don't we just go knock on her door and ask her? I'm sure she'll invite us in for coffee and donuts. We can have a little tête-à-tête. After all he's gone through, I'm sure Giles can't wait to see her again."

"Actually, I tend to agree with Buffy," Giles heard himself saying. "I do think she has some kind of a reason for doing all this and we just don't know what it is."

"What?" Anya looked at him incredulously. "Is my hearing going wonky, or did I just hear you say essentially, 'Oh, it's just that no one understands her'?"

"That's a rather broad way of putting it, but . . . yes, I did say that." Giles realized that now that he was healed, even though he'd never forget, it was actually quite easy to forgive Willow for what she'd done to him. This situation wasn't much different from what he had endured with Angel, although Angel's intentional torture of him had made forgiveness, even *acceptance*, somewhat more difficult. Yet there had been reasons, good ones, why Angel—the real, *souled* Angel—hadn't truly been to blame for that. This situation might be the same, if only they could get to the bottom of it.

"I don't believe what I'm hearing," Anya said. She sounded bitter and angry. "If a man had done that to a woman, and she'd come to me as a vengeance demon, I would have been completely willing to enact whatever retribution she'd asked for. A good option might be taking his skeletal structure and putting it on the outside of his body—"

"There's a vision I didn't need," Xander said, paling a little.

"Yuck," Dawn said.

"Actually," Anya said, "I did that once. It was in the fourteenth century." She'd forgotten her anger for the moment and was smiling a little at the memory. "Medicine during those times was really primitive, and it was a great opportunity for the local self-proclaimed physician to see what was inside the human body."

"Blah," Buffy said. "Can we reroute the conversation back to Riley? This area's getting a little too wet work for me."

"Ditto," Dawn said. "Where were we?"

"Buffy was going to tell Fido-Riley to sit," Xander said helpfully.

"Xander, knock it off," Buffy said. "What if it was you inside a layer of full-body mud?"

"The spa treatment." Xander shrugged. "To be honest? I'm betting he doesn't feel a thing." He tapped the side of his skull. "Involuntary brain responses and nothing else."

Buffy scowled at him, then walked over to the golem and stared up at it. For a moment she didn't seem to know what to do, then she finally just pointed at one of the chairs. "Okay, let's try this. Uh . . . do you want to sit?"

Nothing.

"Try phrasing it as a command rather than a question," Giles suggested. "The creature has extremely limited brain function and apparently no vocal ability at all. It may not actually be able to respond to a question."

"He," Buffy reminded him. "This isn't an it—not completely, anyway. It's Riley."

"Sort of," Dawn said.

"Enough of this," Buffy said stubbornly. "Let's try something else. I will *not* tell him to sit like he's a dog. It's too tacky." She walked to the other side of the room, but made sure to stay within the golem's sight. His eyes tracked her movement, the only thing about him that seemed to be alive at the moment. When she was as far away from him as she could get, she turned around and met the Riley-golem's gaze. "Come," she said.

Xander raised an eyebrow. "Exactly how is 'come' different from 'sit'?"

Buffy ignored him. It took four or five seconds, but the golem finally began to move. It was like watching a stone statue break free of its moorings; the thing was stiff-legged and slow, but it did make its way to where Buffy stood. After the first few steps there was clearly the disconcerting sense that this creature made of dried earth would be nearly unstoppable.

Buffy looked over at Giles. "Okay, now what?"

Giles rubbed his chin. "Try something else," he said. "Just don't make it too complex."

Buffy nodded but looked like she had no idea what to do. Then she glanced at Xander and got a mischievous grin on her face. "Attack Xander," she said.

Xander gaped at her from where he sat. "Hey, not funny, Buff!"

The golem turned and began plodding relentlessly toward Xander.

"Buffy," Giles said sternly. "Do you really think this is a good idea?"

"Oh, boy," Xander said. His chair scraped loudly against the floor as he pushed back from the table. "Let's hope it'll listen to you when you tell it to back off." The golem was about halfway across the room now, heading toward him with single-minded purpose. "A little help here, please!"

Buffy giggled. "Oh, ye of little faith and all that." She raised her voice a little. "Riley, stop."

It took the golem three nerve-wracking steps to stop his forward motion, but ultimately he did come to a clumsy halt.

"Well," Giles said a bit too brightly, "I think we've gotten our questions answered." Xander let out the breath he hadn't realized he'd been holding.

"You guys worry too much," Buffy said. "I knew he would stop."

Anya made a *hmph* sound. "Oh, please. You can't *ever* be sure what a man is going to do," she said darkly.

"Riley's not a man," Dawn said. "He's—"

"Okay, stop right there," Xander interrupted. "I don't know how much of old Riley's thought processes are still processing, but that's getting way too far into the realm of personal insult. Let's not go there and risk making mud-boy *really* mad."

"A fine idea," Giles seconded.

"So," Buffy said, "we think we can control him. Now what do we do with him?"

"I thought we wanted to set him free," Dawn said.

"I mean, we can't have him hanging around for the rest of our lives."

"My thoughts exactly," Xander said, eyeing the golem. "Besides, he makes me nervous."

"I think he makes all of us a bit edgy," Giles said. "And Dawn is right. We should be doing all we can to . . ." He paused, then frowned. He'd been about to say "destroy him," but because somewhere inside the creature was Riley's spirit, there was no way that phrase would ever sound appropriate. "Release his spirit," he finally finished.

"How?" Buffy asked simply.

"Well, let's start by giving him a thorough examination," Giles said. The golem hadn't moved and Giles made his way over there and squinted at it, letting his gaze trace the features that were, the more he looked at it, unmistakably Riley Finn's. "Interesting. Look here." He gestured to the others to come closer, and when they did, Giles pointed at the golem's forehead. "See these letters? They're Hebrew. They're the letters *aleph*, *mem,* and *tav*, which form *emet* and mean 'truth.' Theoretically we should be able to erase this first one, *aleph*, and the golem will die, because that changes the meaning to 'death.' Obviously that breaks the command of life that animated him to begin with, and thereby ends his existence."

"So do it," Dawn said. "End of golem problem, right?"

Giles shook his head. "I'm afraid it's not quite that simple. We'll certainly try it, but I can almost guarantee that these words are not the only thing that animates him."

"'Almost' being the word on which I'm focusing," Xander said enthusiastically. "I know I've asked this before: Do you mean almost as in horseshoes, or almost as in hand grenades?" His mouth turned up in a skittish grin. "I'm only mentioning it because the end result covers a pretty wide range. And there's the off chance that the whole death thing command could mean *cause* it and not *do* it."

Giles frowned. "I'm not sure I follow."

Xander leaned forward. "Here's the thing. Say just for the sake of giggles that we wipe out muddy man's facial tattoo, and say just for the sake of even more giggles that all it does is tick him off. What then?"

Giles's frown deepened. "There wouldn't be any reason for the golem to get angry about that."

"There isn't any reason for a lot of things around here," Dawn said.

"Isn't *that* the truth," Anya muttered.

"It doesn't work that way." Giles folded his arms. "While it's true we've had our share of surprises recently, there are certain laws of the supernatural and the universe that creations such as the golem must follow in order to . . . well, be what they are. I can assure you that over the centuries very little that we've seen or gone up against is new; somewhere, someone has experienced it and written about it." He tapped a stack of books on the table. "It is these experiences that form the basis of modern day knowledge."

"And of course you've read every book on every subject there is to read about everywhere," Dawn said smartly.

Giles lifted his nose. "Well, I wouldn't go *that* far, certainly, but—"

"'Nuff said," Dawn said, with a lift of her own nose.

"I'm just not so sure about wiping part of its face off," Xander insisted. "What if that's like wiping away part of his brain? Like all of a sudden we say 'speak' and he bites instead."

"How many times do I have to tell you he's not a dog?" Buffy demanded crankily.

"I say we try it," Anya said. "Actually, I say *Buffy* tries it. After thinking about it, I agree. This *is* Riley . . . well, sort of . . . that we're talking about. It—he—was ready to do the crash down on us, but he stopped cold at the sight of Buffy. While the golem in him wants to pound anything in sight, clearly the Riley in him doesn't want to hurt Buffy no matter what Willow's orders were."

Buffy studied the Riley golem for a few moments, then shrugged and pushed to her feet. "All right, I'll give it a shot," she said. "I'm with Anya—I just don't think he's going to hurt me."

Xander made a groaning sound in his throat. "Pardon me if I back away," he said. "A *long way* away."

"No problem," Buffy said, and Xander had to marvel silently at how confident she sounded, especially since she was about to do a little more than just steer this mountain-size mud man.

Standing in front of the golem now, Buffy stared up at him. She could see so much of Riley in his features; it amazed her that the others couldn't, or maybe they *wouldn't*. Could that be why they didn't sympathize with his plight the way she did? On the other hand, maybe it was just her imagination, filling in the details because she had known him so well, so intimately. They had looked into each other's eyes, traced the shapes of cheekbones and eyebrows, counted eyelashes and the numbers of colors in each other's irises. The lines on their faces at the time, the lines that they'd imagined would be in the future—they'd known every inch by heart, and it pained Buffy to no end to see those lines here, etched in hard, dried earth—dead earth—on her former lover's face. She *had* loved him, although not as much as he'd wanted her to. It broke her heart to see him like this, to know that this meant the man she'd once held in her arms was truly dead.

For a few moments, Buffy forgot about the others in the room—if they made any sound, she didn't hear it; if they moved into the range of her vision, she didn't see them. All that existed in the world was Riley and her and the deep-seated wish that she could spare him any more misery.

Carefully, she reached up and ran her fingers along the earthen line of his jaw, feeling the grittiness of its surface on the outside while her memory remembered another sensation entirely. She let her fingers linger along his cheek for a couple of seconds, then slid them upward. There was no resistance; the golem didn't move or flinch, and he certainly didn't try to stop her. While the rest of him was dry and hard, the skin across his forehead was surprisingly soft and malleable. When Buffy wiped her thumb across the first letter etched into his forehead, the image easily smoothed out and disappeared.

Still holding her gaze with the Riley golem's, Buffy stepped back and waited.

Nothing happened.

He still stood there, motionless, bright hazel eyes unblinking and fixed steadily on her.

"Well, there you go," Xander said a little too cheerfully.

"Look on the brighter side of the darkness," Dawn said. "At least he's not trying to kill us."

"So he has something additional that animates him," Giles said.

"The backup system," Anya said, and Giles nodded.

Buffy sighed. "So now what? He's stuck this way and we're stuck in a stalemate with Willow?"

Giles pulled off his glasses and wiped them thoughtfully. "Actually, I have a plan. If we can't put him out of commission, we might as well put him to work for us."

Chapter Sixteen

Twilight.

It had become Willow's favorite time, when the daylight was almost gone but the full dark hadn't yet taken over. Grayness settled over everything, softening the stark edges of daylight but still shedding gentle illumination on what could later become the terrifying, often dangerous shadows of the night.

The members of her coven weren't there yet. Most had normal jobs around town, things they did during the day to hide their true natures . . . although, as the Ghost of Tara had suggested sometime ago, Willow's influence over them was changing their existences. How had she put it? Now Willow remembered.

"You're corrupting them."

Willow preferred to think of it as enlightening, show-ing the women a newer, darker path to self-fulfillment.

And wasn't that what it was all about? Her days of self-sacrifice for the good of others were over; those people cared nothing for her personally. Had she not endured the pain of losing the love of her life with barely a nod from her so-called friends? She'd gone through it alone, meted out well-deserved punishment, while listening to nothing but recriminations from Buffy and the others. There had been no understanding, no support—nothing but a few empty words, always colored with caveats about what she *should* be doing instead.

Her coven members? They thought only of themselves, coming here night after night to work for her cause only because they were afraid *not* to. Not even Amy, whom she'd known for years, cared enough about Willow's pain to help just for the sake of helping; she expected to step in as the high-powered replacement when Tara had been resurrected and Willow was done with the whole thing. No, the only person who would think of Willow was Willow, and she'd make damn sure she took very good care of herself from now on.

"They do think of you, you know. Buffy and Giles and the rest of the gang. Xander. They think of you all the time."

Willow turned to face the Ghost of Tara but couldn't help rolling her eyes. "Sure they do. Every moment of every day they think of ways to take me down." She scowled. "I'm not a person to them anymore. I'm a project, something to be worked on and completed."

The Ghost of Tara tilted her head. *"Why do you say that?"*

Willow folded her arms. "Because if they did think of me as a person, they'd realize that I'm still hurting over what happened. And that they're turning on me like they are only makes it hurt worse. Losing you left this huge, festering wound in me, and what do my *friends* do?" She ground her teeth. "Get all righteousy and fair-to-the-world in favor of Warren. They might as well have spread my wound and poured hot sauce in it."

The Ghost of Tara wandered past Willow, running a ghostly forefinger along the edge of a table. There was a light layer of dust on it, the day's accumulation, but her movement never left a mark. *"They don't see it like that,"* she said. *"You know the deal. They think they're doing what's right."*

Willow started to retort, then she stopped and stared at the spirit. Her eyes narrowed. "Wait," she said slowly. "Do you know what they're thinking—Buffy, Giles, all the others?"

The Ghost of Tara looked at her sadly. *"No, Willow. You've got this idea that I'm like the Wonder Woman of the spirit world, but that's just not the way it is. I'm just me."*

Willow's expression softened a little, but she wasn't sure she truly believed the Ghost of Tara. The spirit always seemed to know what Willow was thinking, what she was planning, and it wasn't like psychic phenomena ran on a selective filing system. So—

The Ghost of Tara's voice floated past Willow's ears, surrounding her with sudden warmth and cutting off the notion that she might have been betrayed. *"I know what's in your mind and heart because I love you, Willow."*

Willow pressed her lips together and said nothing. She wanted to believe—so badly—but she couldn't. She needed Tara made *flesh*, not her ghostly substitute. Willow needed to *feel* Tara, her skin, her lips, the pressure of her hand squeezing around hers. How she wished the real Tara were here now.

For a moment, Willow thought she smelled coffee.

She closed her eyes and inhaled, and whether she was really smelling it or not suddenly didn't matter. She wasn't here anymore, in this lavishly appointed Wiccan loft. The people she'd once valued most in the world weren't trying to destroy everything she was trying to do just because they thought she should do what they wanted.

And Tara was alive again.

Okay, so she had the presence of mind to realize it was a memory, but even so, Willow let herself sink fully into it. It was a sweet thing to recall, her and Tara sitting at one of those high, little round cafe tables in the Espresso Pump, leaning toward each other and laughing over something that had happened in one of their classes that morning—Willow couldn't quite get that deeply into it, but whatever the situation had been, they'd both thought it was hilarious. Tara had been wearing one of her usual peasant-style blouses; this one was pale yellow and it had tiny white daisies with bright green centers embroidered all the way around the collar and the loose sleeves. It was new, and Willow had complimented Tara on how nice she looked as they'd left the classroom.

Willow wasn't sure how long she stood there—a

moment, a minute, a half hour—but in that time, she saw, heard, smelled and felt it all: the hot coffee drink with the sweet, melting whipped cream and chocolate sprinkles floating across its surface; the leftover taste of cherries in her mouth from the pastry she and Tara had shared; Tara's delighted laughter tinkling across the table and floating above the surrounding conversation like the notes from a crystal dinner bell. She even felt the fabric of her own clothes brushing against her skin as she reached across the cool surface of the table and took Tara's hand. Tara's skin was warm as it touched hers, and she squeezed—

—and her fingers closed around nothing.

Willow opened her eyes and realized she was crying.

The Ghost of Tara was standing in front of her, her face suffused with sadness as she stared at Willow. Her hand was extended and when Willow looked down, she saw her own fingers, open then closing again reflexively, melting through the gauzy image of the spirit's fingers.

She inhaled sharply. "Was that . . . you?" she whispered. "Did you do that?"

Slowly, the Ghost of Tara nodded. *"Yes,"* she said softly. *"It was me."*

Willow's heart was pounding. "Can we do it again? Please?"

But Tara's spirit only shook her head. *"I'm sorry, baby. We mustn't. You need to . . . face reality."*

Willow swallowed, fighting against the anger that was suddenly sparking inside her. "Why?" she demanded. "What harm could it do?" She paused. "Why would you tease me like that?"

"You can't live in the past, Willow. What you just saw and felt . . ." The spirit hesitated. *"You were in so much pain. I just wanted to relieve it for a little while."*

"So it can come back again when you stop?" Willow whirled and strode to the window, furious. "At least if I knew you would do it again, I'd have something to look forward to."

"I'm not strong enough."

Willow blinked, then frowned and looked back at the spirit. "What?"

The Ghost of Tara lifted one shoulder apologetically. *"My abilities are limited. I'm a newbie."*

Willow stared at her for a moment before understanding. "Fine. And I'm going to see to it that you don't ever turn into a golden oldie."

"Willow—"

"Stop," Willow commanded. "Right now. I'm through arguing about this for now. The others will be here any moment and we have work to do, and I'm not listening to you on this subject anymore." She looked down at a pile of spell books. "I think I'm close," she said. "You know that."

"I know it won't work."

But Willow only lifted her chin. She'd heard all the denials and been through the wins and loses in this game of bringing Tara back to life. Sometimes the Ghost of Tara told her what she needed to hear, sometimes it told her nothing but doom and gloom. She welcomed the spirit's presence, but it did little to actually *help* her. Because of that she could no longer count on the truth of the spirit's words, and she would certainly no longer revolve her plans around what it said. And just in case the Ghost of Tara wasn't particularly into the mind-reading mode right now, Willow decided to say the words out loud.

"I'm sorry," she said simply. "But I just don't believe you anymore."

"Are we ready for this?" Buffy asked.

Xander looked at her unhappily. "As much as we ever are."

Anya elbowed him sharply. "Don't pay any attention to Mr. Disaster here. We can handle this."

Giles looked up at Willow's building and nodded. "Yes," he said. "I believe this time we can—thanks to the golem's help."

Xander looked at the golem doubtfully. It stood next to Buffy like some kind of crumbling stone statue, unmoving and silent. When it did move, it wasn't exactly at the speed of light—it had taken them three times as long to get here with the golem resolutely plodding along after Buffy like an old dog with painful joints.

"Do you think they're up there?" Dawn asked, squinting up. The building looked the same as it always did—no windows, no openings, a quietly beautiful structure in the center of a field of dirty industrial metal.

"Aren't they always?" Anya asked.

Dawn thoughtfully followed Giles's gaze. "I wonder what she's offered them," she said. "There must be something that keeps them coming back night after night. Power? Money?"

"No," Anya said. "I remember what Ross told me before he was killed, that the women he'd been eavesdropping on had talked about the cat demon Willow had created." She shrugged. "It's a roundabout conclusion, but what I pulled from the whole thing was that they didn't agree with what she was doing . . . yet what they thought didn't matter." She paused and gave Giles a meaningful look. "To me that says Willow is using fear as the great motivator."

"Always works for me," Xander put in.

Buffy nodded. "The word at the bar is that she's gotten *extremely* powerful, so we need to be very careful here."

Xander ran a hand through his hair, unwittingly spiking it upward. "So we're doing exactly what right now? Not the same spell as before, right? 'Cause that turned out to be pretty painful on the receiving end, and I thought that wasn't the goal."

"Correct," Giles said. Over one shoulder was a heavy bag, and he shifted under its weight. "Our goal tonight isn't to actually harm anyone. In the best of all possible situations, Buffy would be able to get up there and free both Spike and Oz. However, that's unlikely, given Oz's current werewolf state; she probably won't be able to get anywhere near him. So we send the golem and Buffy up there to keep her busy while I work a little side spell." Giles fixed Buffy with a stern look. "You'll need to be very careful, Buffy. I know you feel you're invincible, but things are no longer equal in that realm. I'm afraid Willow has become quite a bit more powerful than you."

Buffy nodded, but it was clear from her expression that she wasn't at all pleased by Giles's observation.

"I'll need Dawn, Xander, and Anya down here with me to ensure the spell works," Giles said, "so I'm afraid you and the golem will have to go it alone. The golem will only obey you, anyway."

Again, Buffy nodded. "Got it."

"Keep her nice and busy," Anya said. "Tell the big galoot here to have a smash and grab party or whatever, but *don't* let Willow relax long enough to turn her attention on us. We have to be left alone for this to work. One distraction and"—Anya snapped her fingers—"the results last about as long as that."

Giles dug into his bag and started bringing out his artifacts. "All right," he said. "Time to take a little something out of Willow's hands and return the odds to our favor."

"Here's what we're going to do," Willow told the gathered women of her coven. They stared back at her with no attempt to disguise the resentment in their gazes. Willow could understand it; after forcing them to work for her under threat of pain or worse, she'd first failed to protect them, then lost the battle to destroy the enemy who'd nearly decimated them to begin with.

Too bad. She wasn't standing up here to win any popularity contests.

"I am tired," she continued, "of wasting my energy on Buffy and her cohorts." Her black gaze turned to them all. "And the 'my' part of what I just said? It includes your energy, all the power that you're gathering for me so I can bring Tara back." She leaned forward over the table in front of her. "Your energy is *my* energy. So we're going to forget them for now and focus on what I wanted to do in the first place." She stood up straight again. "We're going to suck this town dry of every bit of power we can find. *No exceptions.* And we start tonight. We—"

"You're a fool if you think they'll leave us alone," Anan interrupted. Her voice was flat and brittle.

"I didn't ask for your opinion," Willow said icily. "And I'm tired of hearing it. You are *very* expendable. Interrupt me again and I will lay you out next to your precious Flo—permanently."

The women seated on either side of Anan shifted uncomfortably, trying to surreptitiously put distance between themselves and her, just in case. Anan's return look at Willow was filled with acid, but this time she held her tongue.

"Now that *that's* all settled," Willow said with false cheerfulness, "we're finally going to take our search for power more personally. There are other places to—"

At the far end of the loft, the door that led to the maze-filled first floor exploded inward.

As Willow gaped at what was coming through the door, the Ghost of Tara slid up to her and whispered in her ear.

"*Sometimes it is not the force of will that moves the mountain, but the force of love.*"

The Riley-golem had finally come back home.

Chapter Seventeen

Whatever protection spell Willow had placed on the door to her loft didn't matter. Perhaps because the golem was Willow's own creation, he went through it like it was made of butter. Once he was inside the loft, there was no time for thought or decisions. The golem plowed through everything in sight—people, furniture, *anything*—with a ferocity that Buffy found instantly terrifying. She couldn't stop him, though; the second she followed him through the doorway, Willow focused on her and left the other members of the coven to deal with her mud-man creation.

"*You!*" Willow shrieked. "It's always *you*, isn't it, Buffy? You have to screw up every, single thing in my life!"

Already objects were flying through the air, and Buffy couldn't tell whether they were being thrown by human hand, golem, or magical direction. A chair that should have been far too heavy for anyone normal to pick up somersaulted toward her head, and she ducked, then rolled under a shelf full of exploding glass bottles and vials.

"Willow, stop!" Buffy shouted, but Willow wasn't listening. "Stop it! We just want you to not—"

The couch, a heavy and overstuffed thing covered in rich, red fabric, lifted four inches off the floor, but it hung there and spun ominously only long enough for Willow to have her say. "Oh, you *want*, do you?" Willow's voice was full of venom. "You *always* want, Buffy. 'Do this for me, Willow,'" she mimicked. "'And this, too. Oh, and by the way, while you're busy with all that, your lover is going to *die* because some circuit-brained psychopath has it out for *me*.'"

Buffy gasped, then flung herself to the side as the sofa zoomed toward her head. "Willow, that's not fair!" she cried. She caught a glimpse of the Riley-golem on the other side of the room; he was in a whirl-wind of breaking glass and wood, but she was too far away to order him to stop and besides, if she did, that would put Giles and his spell in danger. In another instant, she saw the golem brutally backhand one of the coven members; her limp body soared across the room and crashed against the opposite wall.

Oh, no.

"You're damned right, it's not fair!" Willow screamed. The stridency, the pure fury, in Willow's voice was enough to yank Buffy's attention back to her. *"It's all your fault, Buffy!* Everything I did was for you, until Tara came along and showed me that it was time I found a life for *me* . . . and for her! And then, *bang!* The woman I loved, who never did *anything* to you, *DIES BECAUSE OF YOU!*" She was bellowing now, so angry that a wind had risen up around her and pushed her ink-colored hair straight back from her face.

"Willow, *stop*!" Buffy cried. "That's not true—"

"Isn't it? *Isn't* it?" Oblivious to the carnage around her, Willow came forward through a swirl of flying objects. "Then you tell me why Tara deserved to die when Warren wanted to kill *you*!"

Buffy's mouth worked, but where were the words to answer a question like that? The thing was, Willow's tirade seemed a little too close to the bone for comfort. Had her words always been like that, because now suddenly Buffy felt suffused with guilt, overrun by it, choked by her own guilty conscience? There were so many what-ifs in the world. Was Tara's death truly nothing more than one of those? *What if* Tara had been in a different part of the house? Or *what if* Buffy hadn't let Warren get away after beating him nearly senseless at the carnival the night before he'd shown up in her yard with a gun?

Well, hey—that wasn't all that hard to answer, now was it?

And adding to that, off to the side, the Riley-golem was destroying everything in its path . . . including people.

Willow was almost on top of her now, and some instinct for self-preservation kicked in and saved Buffy's butt just as Willow swung a clawed hand at her head. Normally it wouldn't have been any big deal, except on this one it looked very much like Willow's fingers were made of steel, and the steel itself was on fire. Buffy ducked under the blow and rolled, getting her arms scraped badly by the pieces of shattered glass that were everywhere.

There were certain situations where being at floor level was a good thing and generally meant you were safe. Not here, with the Riley golem thundering around like some kind of doomified King Kong and Willow bearing down on her. Suddenly Buffy wanted to be anywhere else in the world. She needed to get to that golem and stop him. How typically occult that the commands she'd given him as she pointed toward the door downstairs had not been specific enough. The golem was like a galloping deal with the devil that had come back to bite the maker on the butt.

"Get us in here, and smash everything in sight."

It had seemed so simple at the time, but that was just it—it was *too* simple and completely lacking in the kind of clarity that was essential here. The proof was obvious: The limited intelligence creature powered by Riley's spirit had taken it to mean that it should basically eliminate everything except for Buffy—alive or not—in the room. It was the world's biggest blunder, or, as Willow had just pointed out, maybe it simply came down to Buffy's bad influence over everything with which she came in contact.

She couldn't worry about Willow right now; she had to get over and stop the golem before he hurt anyone else, before he got to Spike and Oz, neither of whom had a chance in hell of defending himself. There were already bodies everywhere, and from the looks of the still, crumpled forms, Buffy had a really bad and black feeling about the outcome of tonight's overbroad battle strategy.

She started to scramble to her feet, then Buffy felt herself being lifted into the air. Boy, she really hated being puppetized, especially by someone who wasn't really viewing her as the current favorite in the playtime marionette collection. Up and up and up, until finally her head bonked hard against the way-too-high ceiling. "Ow!"

"Haven't you learned yet, Buffy?" Willow called. "Or do you *ever* learn?"

Buffy swallowed. Willow—and the floor—were an awfully long way down. "Will," she said. "I'm sorry. All I can say is it wasn't intentional—"

"Is it ever?" Willow demanded, glaring up at her. "Do you think that somehow makes it *all right*?"

"No, of course not—"

"Maybe," Willow said with sudden, ominous calm, "I've been planning all this time to punish the wrong people."

Buffy opened her mouth, but honestly? She couldn't think of a single thing to say to that. Oh, there were a thousand protests, sure, but then there was that little part of her that wondered, again, if maybe Tara's death really was her fault after all.

Willow smiled blackly. "Hit a nerve there, didn't I? The Big Bad Slayer, savior of Sunnydale and the average Jack and Jill in distress. Maybe we should rename you. Call you something entirely different, like 'The Queen of It's Not My Fault.'"

Buffy started to answer, then gasped as she saw the golem out of the corner of her eye, just as the werewolf version of Oz leaped for its throat—

—and the Riley golem caught it by the neck in midair.

"All right," Giles whispered to the others, "we have to be extremely cautious here. It's best for everyone involved if Willow never realizes that we're outside the door."

"Yeah, you're not kidding," Xander said, but his voice was at the same muffled volume level. "Not to reopen an old wound, but I don't think any of us wants to try the wheelchair route."

"No," Giles agreed. "Believe me, you don't." He gave them all a meaningful glance, then looked up the poorly lit expanse of battered stairway above them. The golem had cut the path for them, opting for the sheer destruction method through the maze of mirrors that had dumbfounded Buffy on her first attempt to get upstairs. He wondered what Buffy had told the golem to do, but from the sound of the fight going on upstairs, he was afraid to find out. He should have given her better direction, or even told her exactly what to say. A poorly worded instruction to a creature with that much strength could be devastating. Now it could well be too late.

He shook himself back to the here and now. Hindsight and the I-should-haves were wonderful things, but he needed to focus. "We have to stay out of sight," he said. "I need two people to help me perform the trapping spell, and one person to be our eyes."

"That would be me," Dawn offered. "Eyes all the way. I've got it covered."

Giles nodded, but it took a few moments of them staring expectantly at him before he could say, "Excellent. Then let's go on up." He tried to look and sound confident, but he was having just a bit of difficulty with the façade. See, he wasn't exactly afraid of Willow.

He was terrified.

She had, he supposed, given him the worst beating of his life. Only the soulless Angel had hurt him more, and that, Giles supposed, was only because at the time he hadn't had the luxury of paralysis to deaden the nerve endings while Angel had had a jolly good time playing torturer at Giles's expense. Giles couldn't quite find it in himself to be grateful, though; while the paralysis may have been a little on the sanity saving side at the time, the end result had been far more devastating.

Walking up the steps, just the simple act of putting one foot in front of the other took everything Giles had. He found everything narrowing down to that one, tiny thing—the act of lifting one foot, then forcing the other to pick itself up and continue. Place, balance, push, and lift. Place, balance, push, and lift. It wasn't until Giles had finally gotten out of that hated wheelchair that he'd realized there was so much to be appreciated about doing something as seemingly simple as climbing stairs.

The closer he got to the top of the staircase, the

more Giles could see and hear the chaos that was happening on the other side of that doorway; the more he saw and heard, the harder Giles's heart pounded in his chest. Louder and louder, until the sound of his own hammering heartbeat was so absurdly tremendous in his own ears that it actually drowned out the screams and the crashes and the hellish windstorm only a few feet away.

Stop it!

A mental command to himself, heard by no one but Giles. Willow wasn't going to see him, wouldn't even know he was there, outside the doorway. And even if she did, so what? He couldn't let his mind, his life, his entire future *existence*, be ruled by fear. He wouldn't be like Andrew and Jonathan, out somewhere in the world and on the run because of their terror, perhaps for the rest of their lives. He *wouldn't*.

And then they were at the top of the stairs and peering fearfully around the doorway's edge as they hurriedly set up what they needed to do Giles's spell.

Willow didn't so much throw Buffy down as drop her.

Buffy had time to be surprised, again, that the floor looked so far away, then she hit the wood with enough of a thud that the fall momentarily knocked the wind out of her. She groaned and for a few seconds forgot about everything else in the room; extended memory lapses were, alas, a luxury that currently did not exist in her life.

Buffy hauled air into her bruised lungs, then pushed herself to a sitting position. Everything around her was in chaos—broken furniture, shattered glass, papers, trinkets, books, you name it. There was crying, moaning, and screaming, but it was all mixed up and she couldn't tell where which was coming from. She wanted to stand but one of her legs hurt too much—was it broken? Probably just sprained, and if she could stay off of it for a few minutes, her Slayer constitution would no doubt push it enough toward healing to where she'd be able to walk again, or at least passably lurch. This was twice that she had gotten her hind end royally kicked by facing off with Willow, and as far as she was concerned, that was twice too many.

But there was no time to dwell on that. Right now, there was a pile of fabric about four yards away that looked suspiciously like a person. Buffy crawled toward it after a cautious glance over her shoulder; so far, so good—over by the fireplace, the golem was doing a bang-up job of keeping Willow nice and busy.

Were Giles and the others where they were supposed to be? Buffy sure hoped so, since this whole thing was engineered for that purpose, but she was going to have to let them do their part; right now, the woman on the floor in front of her looked pretty beaten up.

Buffy crab-crawled for the last foot or so, then reached out and shook the woman's shoulder. "Hey," she whispered. "Can you hear me? Are you all . . ."

Her words faded away as Buffy's grasp rolled the figure toward her. Once a lovely young woman with ebony skin and dark chocolate eyes, one side of her face was now nearly crushed. Her mouth hung open and blood had flooded her lifeless eye sockets; still, her final stare pinned Buffy in place and washed her in guilt.

"Oh!" Buffy's hand flew to her mouth and she bit down on her own knuckle to keep from making any more noise. Dear God, she'd never meant for any of these women to *die*. She and the rest of the Scooby gang hadn't even been sure they were evil. What had she done?

The battle behind her was peaking, the golem and Willow locked in combat, but Buffy couldn't be concerned about that now. There were more piles of fabric scattered around the room, more of the coven's members crushed and brought down by the so-foolish and overly broad command she'd given the golem. As she staggered from one body to the next and the next, Buffy railed at herself. How could she have been so stupid? Here was an all-too-familiar face, Amy Madison, unconscious and battered but thankfully still breathing. Even amid the chaos, Willow's words—

"It's all your fault, Buffy!"

—jumped back into her mind with razorlike pain.

And here . . . God. It was another dead woman. Blond hair, the glint of blue going dull behind eyelids that hadn't quite closed. Buffy knew this one, too— Anan. She'd come to the Magic Box seeking revenge because her loved one had ended up comatose, thanks to Giles's relocation spell. That, Buffy realized, would be the auburn-haired woman lying in the sleeping area who'd stayed oblivious to everything around her.

Would these people have really died if Buffy had just stayed away and left Willow *alone*, as she'd wanted?

She'd never know, and now it was far, far too late.

It just aggravated the crap out of her that her demonic creatures kept turning on her.

Willow let Buffy drop and at the same time brought her right hand down in a chopping motion while glaring at the golem and Oz. The left hand the golem had wrapped around the werewolf's throat separated neatly from its wrist as an invisible shield slammed into place between the two of them. Oz, stretched to the limit of his chain, jerked up and onto his hind legs; disconnected from its main body, the golem's hand contorted and released, flying into the air as Oz snarled and snapped. Like a well-trained dog jumping for a frisbee, the werewolf caught it neatly between its heavy, drooling jaws. When Oz clamped down, the hand cracked and turned to dust, filling Oz's mouth with a dry pile of dirt that made him sneeze and shake his head furiously as he backed away.

For a moment the Riley-golem only stared dumbly at the werewolf, not understanding why he couldn't get to it anymore. Then, finally realizing the loss of his appendage, the golem brought the injured arm up and stared at it. Pushing her thoughts of Buffy aside as she strode across the room, Willow had to marvel at this thing she herself had made; by the time she got within three feet of the golem, his hand had almost fully grown back.

"Well," Willow said irritably, "you really do work

well. It's just a shame you don't work for *me* anymore."

The Riley-golem looked from his hand—nearly complete now—to her, then its normally bland face twisted in such a look of black hatred that Willow actually stepped back. Her mouth tightened as she stared at it. How typical—yet another person, no matter what form he took, in her life that was up for abandoning her in favor of the all-righteous Buffy. It was always all about Buffy. What the hell was it about that Super Bitch that made this such the fashionable thing? She started to say something to that effect—not that this idiot mound of dried mud would actually understand or be able to answer her—when the creature swung its fully formed fist into the side of her head and knocked her nearly clear across the loft.

Willow landed awkwardly, with her legs all twisted up in the folds of her heavy velvet robes, and her head throbbing painfully. "Enough of *this*," she snarled, and ripped the fabric aside. It always paid to dress sensibly, and while she'd enjoyed playing Wiccan Princess every so often over the last weeks, now it was time to roll up her sleeves and go for the down and dirty.

Under the robes she was wearing black jeans and a snug-fitting black denim top with free-flowing sleeves. Now Willow rose more than stood, ready to face the creature of her own making. The golem had either forgotten about Oz or it didn't care anymore; now it was striding toward her with obvious single-minded purpose: to destroy her.

In the five seconds it took the golem to cross the distance between her and it, time slowed to enough of a crawl to let Willow see the whole picture. There was Spike to one side of the fireplace, currently still nothing more than a useless piece of former-bloodsucking mental mush. On the other side of the fancy stonework was the werewolf version of Oz—quite the entertaining bad-attitude puppy, and she liked him a lot. That and the good memories of the past had been enough to make her step in and prevent his addition to the body count.

Speaking of body count, her slow motion scan chalked up two of the totally dead kind, and Willow felt the slow simmer of anger inside her ramp up to full boil. Njeri and Anan were history, and while the two of them hadn't exactly been stellar on Willow's obedience and behavior chart, they *had* been quite powerful. With the sole exception of the oblivious Flo, every single one of the others was, in one way or another, hurt, and some of the injuries were critical. In fact the only one who wasn't knocked senseless—or worse—was Ena; while the dark Celtic witch had an arm broken in two places—boy, that had to hurt—she was appropriately furious . . . and she was headed straight for Buffy. Excellent.

And, of course, Willow could *feel* Giles and the rest of his little tribe of mystical wannabes right outside the door. There was Anya, who couldn't make up her mind whether she should be a demonic bad girl or Xander's mistress and house-mouse; Xander himself, of course, the perpetual clunky screw-up whose only saving grace was that he could pound a nail into a piece of wood without bending the metal; and Dawn, who as far as Willow was concerned was nothing more than the wishful thinking of a bunch of holy men with a dose of extra-strong willpower. Before this was all over, Willow was going to show them some *real* willpower.

And Giles . . . ah, now *he* was amusing. The old librarian was reeking with overflowing emotions, exuding everything from fear to regret to I-can-still-somehow-save-her self-righteousness. Everything coming out of him had all the pleasantness of an overly strong onion.

Please.

Willow's little slow-mo timeshift abruptly ended, and then there was no more time to think about Giles and the others, or what reason they might have to be hovering just outside her door. She and the Riley-golem came together in a hurricane of fists and rage and, let's face it, Willow was getting on the down side of the physical. It hardly seemed to notice when she hit it, and despite the intensified zing of her Wiccan powers, she was taking the old three steps back for every one step gained—one good crack to the golem's head got her whaled on at least three times. Since giving up wasn't an option—this mound of earthworm-ridden dirt would end up killing her if she did—Willow just kept at it, until finally she found herself face to face with the golem and wrapped in a heavy and exceedingly painful bear hug.

"Oh, great!" she gasped, but there wasn't a whole

lot of room for inhalation to keep talking. The Riley-golem had managed to corner her and get his arms under hers, tight around her ribs. In fact she had a pretty good bet that the bones were going to crack not very far up the clock. "Let . . . me . . . go!"

The golem didn't, of course. Willow wheezed and stared into the golem's impassive hazel eyes, trying to mentally command it to release her. Nothing. Her vision darkened at the edges and her head rolled, but she fought the urge to surrender to the oncoming unconsciousness. She *had* to get out of this creature's hold. She *had* to!

It was a futile movement, but she brought her arms up and pushed at his shoulders anyway. Then it dawned on her—his face was so close that even through the black and yellow sparkles starting to dance across her vision, she could see the uneven smudge across his forehead where the *aleph* had been wiped away, obviously in a failed attempt by Giles and the others to put the Riley-golem out of commission. Despite her predicament, Willow had to smile as she forced her hand up and formed her fingers back into sharp-nailed claws. If only they'd known how close they'd been to being able to do just that.

Willow stiffened her fingers and plunged them through the side of the golem's cheek.

Chapter Eighteen

"**S**he knows we're here, Giles. I know she does!"

Anya's urgent voice was supposed to make him work faster, but it only made the librarian more prone to making mistakes. The things he was working with—the wallet-sized photograph of Tara, the small crystal bottle with its matching stopper, and a scrap of material off one of Tara's sweaters that Buffy had found at the bottom of a hamper next to the washing machine—jittered in his suddenly ice-cold fingers. He *had* to be careful, *had* to get this right. Dropping the tear-shaped crystal jar and breaking it, even nicking its rim, would ruin everything, and from what was happening on the other side of this doorway, he knew they would never get another chance to try again.

Speaking of never getting another chance, where the heck was Tara's spirit? For the spell to work, her spirit had to be within viewing range, because at the instant he vocalized the final line, he was supposed to lock eyes with her. There would be no running—if she were within a quarter mile range, the first part of his spell would immobilize her, but obviously that wasn't going to be of much help if he couldn't actually *see* her.

"What are you waiting for?" Dawn hissed. The teenager was so frightened she was actually crowding him, making it difficult for Giles to work in the small space, unwittingly increasing the already nearly suffocating tension he was feeling.

"I can't see Tara," Giles whispered back. "I need to have her in my line of vision before I can start the spell or it won't work!"

Xander elbowed him sharply, making Giles gasp. The younger man's fear was making him put more *oomph* into the move than was necessary. "There," he said under his breath. He gestured toward their right. "At the end of the windows."

Giles jerked around, then grimaced with satisfaction. The Ghost of Tara wasn't that far away from them, far closer than he would have dared hope. At the same time, she didn't appear to be paying any mind at all to Giles and his companions. Instead the spiritual version of the young woman they'd all known was hovering above one of the bodies and gazing unhappily at the others spread around the loft. It was completely focused on the carnage that had been wrought by the Riley golem and, perhaps, on the pounding that Buffy was no doubt going to experience if they didn't all get this over with and get the hell out of here.

Giles took a deep breath and spoke the first line of the spell.

"Bound are you now, Tara, unable to move, unable to flee."

Only twenty feet away, the Ghost of Tara's eyes widened and shock suddenly flashed across her gossamer face. She opened her mouth but nothing came out—no protest, no cry for help. Giles knew it would be the same in the realm of her thoughts; she was as paralyzed in the psychic realm as she was now in the physical, and the Ghost of Tara could think but not project those mental words to Willow.

She was, in a word, alone.

Her expression still incredulous, the Ghost of Tara slowly turned toward Giles and stared at him.

The librarian found himself wanting to scan the loft, desperate to know where Willow was and if she'd noticed them. Was she even now striding toward him, preparing to inflict some grievous injury that this time could never be healed?

But no, he couldn't let himself dwell on that, could not allow his body's fear factor to overrule the irrefutable calculations and conclusions his brain was telling him: They *had* to entrap Tara, no matter what the cost.

Staring at the Ghost of Tara, Giles couldn't help grimacing. No matter what the cost—had he really thought that? Tell that to the young women lying motionless around the room; he had the horrid suspicion that several of them, possibly all, were dead. It was a crushing thing to contemplate. Was what they were about to do really worth that kind of price?

He just wasn't sure.

But he still had to try.

With his gaze still locked with the spirit's, Giles raised the small crystal jar to where the Ghost of Tara couldn't help but see it. The disbelieving look on the nebulous surface of her lovely young face turned to one of dismay as she realized what he was about to do, but he also knew that unless Willow redirected her energies toward him, there was nothing the spirit could do to stop what was going to happen.

"What's Willow doing?" he asked urgently. For a moment he got no answer, then Dawn's shaking voice, barely audible, worked its way into his hearing. "I think she . . . she just killed the mud-thing that held Riley's spirit," she said. There was a beat of silence, then Dawn spoke again, sounding a little more surprised. "Wow—that was messy. I thought only vampires turned to dust."

"You'd better hurry and finish up, Giles," Anya said. "I'm thinking we have . . . what? Maybe ten seconds before Willow bull's-eyes on us again." She tugged at his sleeve. "Come on, Giles."

"Right." He swallowed, still pinning the Ghost of Tara in place with his gaze. *"Drawn into this crystal and held there by me."* As he stared at her, Tara's ghost shuddered, as if the spirit had suddenly been wrapped in a cold, cold wind. *"No matter who tries, your essence is trapped,"* Giles rushed on. Using only one hand, he rolled the photograph small enough to push it through the narrow neck of the crystal jar, all the while struggling to keep his voice slow enough to enunciate the words clearly. Not far away, Tara's spiritual form began a sluggish twist, like a slow-motion hurricane being pulled apart by forces unseen. If Willow turned and saw her now—but no. In just a flicker of his peripheral vision, he could see that she was still over by Oz and the fireplace, distastefully brushing away the layer of dust that had blasted over her in the Riley-golem's final moments.

He shoved the tiny piece of sweater inside the jar and triumphantly stage-whispered the final line of the enchantment. *"Only I can release, my spell be unwrapped!"*

It wouldn't be until later that the four of them would realize how undramatic and anticlimactic the final part of the spell had actually been. Experience had taught them to expect the worst—lots of screaming and noise and wind, especially in those times (like now) when all they really wanted was to do the abra-cadabra and get the hell out. This time fate seemed to be on their side; maybe it was the universe itself that didn't like what Willow was doing or was going to do, or just flat wanted to give Willow a smack or two on the hand for being so naughty, because there was nothing but a swift, low-key flash of light—in fact it was a lot like a candle being blown out—and then the crystal jar in Giles's palm suddenly wasn't clear anymore. Instead it was filled with a vaguely golden sort of . . . cloud, very soft and fuzzy at the edges. Without pausing to question their good fortune, Giles yanked a small cork from his pocket and pushed it solidly into place. On the other side of the loft, Willow had missed the whole spell, and he wasn't about to tempt fate by sticking around until she got her focus back. "Let's go," he said simply.

"Better words have never tickled my eardrums," Xander muttered. He spun back toward the doorway without waiting for Giles to elaborate, simultaneously pushing Dawn in front of him while yanking Anya along. "I thought we'd *never* get out of here!"

There had been plenty of times in her life when straits had been more dire, but right about now Buffy couldn't recall any. There wasn't much filling her head except the ticked-off Wiccan woman heading her way. Buffy gritted her teeth and stood, ready to meet her, then changed her mind and dropped back to the floor at the last second; all in all, it was a pretty good choice, since it made the energy ball that suddenly flared skim over her scalp. Her hair got a good dose of heat, but hey—at least she still had her head.

Then Buffy was up and diving toward her attacker before the witch could send another head shot her way, crashing into the woman and taking her down in a good, old-fashioned football tackle. There was nothing graceful or high-style movie about it; the two of them went down in a twisted pile of arms and legs, and then they each started punching at each other in earnest.

Any other time, Buffy could have taken it *and* given back three times what she got. But tonight . . . not a chance. Sure, Willow had worked her over good, but it wasn't just that. It wasn't just tonight. It was tonight *and* the time before. Between Willow and her nasty blue cat-demon, Buffy had nearly once again swaggered through the metaphysical equivalent of the great pearly gates. The physical was wearing her down, but the mental part was killing her.

She lashed out with a fist, but her blow was weak and all but ineffective, glancing off the other woman's shoulder and barely making her pause. In return, Buffy got a wallop of a blow to the right side of her jaw, hard enough to make her see stars and rocket pain through the lower part of her face. She was no quitter, but in a moment of nasty clarity, Buffy finally realized that if she didn't get the hell out of here, she might very well die tonight inside the wreckage of Willow's loft.

She managed to duck the next blow and got a precious two seconds to get her bearings and figure out what to do. She hoped to God that Giles and the others had done what they'd come here for, because now there was only one way out of here. Sometimes the most important decisions in life had to be made super fast and on the fly.

Literally.

"She should have been down here by now," Dawn hissed. "Something's wrong!"

The four of them were crouched behind the dubious cover of a small delivery truck parked about fifty feet down the street from Willow's building. Every now and then one of them would pop their head around the corner of it, trying to see whatever was worth viewing. That in itself had a big dose of adventure—every time one of them did it, they felt like one of those pop-up targets in a carnival shooting gallery. One on-the-money shot by Willow or one of her crony Wiccans and someone else would definitely get the prize.

"What happened to the Master of Mud himself?" Xander demanded. "The golem was supposed to protect her, Giles. If we have to go back in there, we're in deep—"

The rest of Xander's statement was cut off by an explosion of glass down the street. They all jumped and crowded together at the corner of the truck, trying to see . . . then wished they hadn't.

"Oh, my," Anya marveled. "Buffy is certainly going to hurt when she—"

Crash!

"—lands," she finished, then drew her lips back in a sympathetic wince. "Ooh."

Xander didn't wait for instructions. He darted forward and Dawn gasped in surprise as he dragged her with him, pulling her across the street in a fast and low military run. Together they zipped over to where Buffy's still body lay amidst a pile of jagged-edged pieces of glass. He felt like Henny Penny, running scared and constantly looking up at the sky, waiting for it—or in this case, Willow—to fall hard on them.

For a heart-stopping moment, when he and Dawn scrambled up next to her, he actually thought Buffy was dead. She was so *still*, so completely and utterly without motion, that his brain told him that somehow this went beyond unconscious. He wasn't the only one, either; he saw every bit of his terror reflected in Dawn's widened eyes as she stared at her sister. Then, as Buffy groaned and pulled in air, that awful impression was gone and replaced by the hard and nasty face of her reality-based pain.

Xander glanced reflexively overhead again and thought he saw movement at the window from which Buffy had taken her swan dive. Not good. "Buffy, come on. Get on your feet," he said urgently. He could feel her pain, he really could, but now was not the time to be empathetic. "We have to get back to the Magic Box. It's not safe here."

Her eyelids fluttered open, but any recognition was replaced by agony. Buffy's face twisted and she tried to push herself up using the arm folded underneath her side—big mistake. Whatever was going on bone-wise inside the skin was enough to actually make her *scream*. Just as quickly as the sound started, it stopped . . . thanks to Dawn slapping her hand over Buffy's mouth. "Shhhhh!"

Buffy shook her face away from Dawn's hand, then ground her teeth against screaming again and rolled onto her back to take her weight off her injured left arm. It didn't look good: From just below the elbow halfway to her shoulder was a deep, purplish bruise that encircled the entire arm and the whole thing was swollen to three times its normal size. "Broken," Buffy gasped. "Really broken this time!"

"Come on," Xander said. He ducked down and slid her right arm over his shoulder, then lifted until her body came with his. It was hard, because she was almost dead weight. Dawn hovered on Buffy's left side, wanting to help but not knowing how to do so without squeezing Buffy's broken arm. "We'll get you to the hospital. We'll get you anywhere but here. *Quick.*"

And they dragged Buffy into the shadows as far away and fast as they could.

Chapter Nineteen

"**H**ere." Giles yanked one of the chairs away from the table. "Right here."

Xander staggered forward and, with Dawn's help, set Buffy on the chair. Freed of her weight, he straightened up and almost lost his balance; her knees had buckled only a block from Willow's loft, so he'd carried her the rest of the way, thinking longingly of that wheelchair that Giles had left back at the shop. If they'd have passed by a grocery shop, he would have snagged a cart and loaded her into it, but no such luck.

Buffy's head lolled backward and Dawn caught it automatically, not liking the slack-muscled way it rolled. She might be the Slayer, but tonight she looked like she'd been run over by a truck, with bruises and scrapes all over her face and arms, not to mention the internal rearrangement of that left one. God, was there more going on inside her? Some other kind of internal injury or another broken bone?

Buffy's eyes opened and she made an effort to pick up her head. She managed to hold it upright for a few moments, then let her chin slump forward and rest on her chest. "Tired," she whispered. "I'm just so *tired.*"

Still clutching the crystal jar that held Tara's spirit, Giles came forward and frowned down at her. "You took more than the average beating, Buffy. Back in front of Willow's, Xander told me he mentioned taking you to the hospital. I think that's probably the best avenue."

"No." Her voice sounded like something that had been run across a cheese grater. "Can't . . . explain . . . this."

Anya stepped in front of Buffy and studied her. "I think we could. We'll say you were a hit and run victim, struck by a large vehicle driven by an ancient person. They're always running people over."

Buffy managed to raise her head again, and this time, actually shake it. "No."

Giles knelt in front of her. "Buffy, your arm looks extremely bad. I'd wager it needs an x-ray so that it can be properly set, and that in itself is going to be very painful. You'll need something to control the pain, the swelling—"

Buffy sat up a little more, blinking to clear her vision. She was actually upright on the chair now, balancing without any help. "I said no."

"But your arm—"

"—will be fine," she finished for him. Before Giles

or any of the others in the room realized what she was going to do, Buffy reached over and gripped her left forearm with her right hand, then gave her broken arm a vicious downward jerk.

Dawn wasn't sure at first if Buffy passed out or not, because her own vision went gray when all the color disappeared from her sister's face. Even Buffy's lips went pale; she looked like a zombie, except that the only thing still alive and wide with shock were her hazel eyes. They were bulging, wider and wider, and now Buffy's mouth was turning red, deep blood red, because she'd clamped down on her own bottom lip to keep herself from crying out. She slumped sideways in the chair, now with both her arms—broken and unbroken—hanging limply at her sides.

"Oh, man," Xander said. He staggered a bit and his own face had paled, leaving his skin looking like chalk dust beneath his dark hair. "That *had* to hurt."

"Is she awake?" Anya asked. "Maybe we should boil some water. That's what they always do in the movies when someone's injured."

"And do what with it?" Dawn asked. She rolled her eyes, then rubbed her hand across her mouth. Her voice was shaking. "I can't believe you didn't learn more than that in all those hundreds of years. She needs something cold to bring down the swelling." She turned and hurried back to the small chest freezer in the back. In less than two minutes she was back and holding out a bundled-up towel.

Anya stared at it suspiciously. "Dawn, what's that? I don't recall us having any ice."

"We don't," Dawn said nonchalantly. "But I found a big frozen snake. I had to break it into a bunch of pieces to make it fit in the bag, though. I hope it wasn't anything important."

Anya's look of dismay was hard to miss. "Important? It's only a Fea's Viper. They're from China and they're very rare." She blinked. "And poisonous."

Dawn shuddered a little bit, then lifted her chin and carefully placed the towel package against the misshapen flesh of Buffy's arm. "Well, it was dead already, plus I broke it into six . . . maybe seven pieces. I don't think it's coming back from the dead now."

"You never know," Anya said ominously. "The snake had been enchanted so that it would come back to life if it was thawed. You can't use a dead snake in a spell. Everyone knows that."

Dawn's mouth dropped open and she yanked the cold wad off Buffy's arm. "This thing is going to come back to life? Why didn't you tell me that?"

Anya shrugged again. "Actually, I'm not sure it will. It was *supposed* to, but then that was before you turned it into a bunch of puzzle pieces. Now I don't know what's going to happen."

"Oh, for crying out loud!" Dawn was just standing there, gaping at Anya, and Xander snatched the damp package away from her. "I'm putting this back in the freezer before we end up having to go out for an antivenom cocktail." He marched back to the freezer and opened the case, then opened the towel and let the plastic bag inside it drop in. He could have sworn he saw the bag squirm before he hurriedly closed the lid.

"But what are we going to use for ice?" Dawn demanded when he got back to the group. "You heard what Giles said—this time it's really bad."

"Not so bad."

Dawn jumped and turned with the rest of them to where Buffy had opened her eyes and was looking at them. Her left arm was still hanging at her side, but she managed to use the right one to straighten herself on the chair and find some semblance of a balanced position.

"Hey," Dawn said softly. She went over and knelt in front of Buffy. "How are you doing? How's your arm?"

"Pretty damned painful," Buffy admitted. She looked down at her hand and the others followed suit; the bruising had crept all the way down to her wrist, leaving an ugly trail of dark red where blood had gathered under the skin. But amazingly, Buffy managed to flex her fingers, although she couldn't do it with any kind of strength. Gingerly she reached down and lifted the arm by the wrist, then carefully placed it across her lap. The movement made air hiss through her teeth, but at least she didn't pass out again. "Even so, I think I'm gonna live."

"I'm thinking a splint would be a good idea," Xander said.

"Yes," Giles agreed. "Keep the arm immobilized, at least until we're sure there's no permanent damage."

"Plaster of Paris," Anya said suddenly. "We have some, I'm sure. I've used it to make images of—"

"The fabric kind will do quite nicely," Giles interrupted. "I see no need to make Buffy into the evening's sculpture project."

"Bandages, then." Anya hurried behind the counter. She rummaged around for a few seconds, then triumphantly held up a double handful of gauzy rolls and packages. "We have lots. Around here it's always a good idea to stock them. Now, what are you going to do about *her*?" Anya asked, pointing at the tear-shaped jar. "One mini-leak, and *poof*—the spirit's out of the bag—so to speak."

"The first thing—"

"Jar," Xander corrected, cutting off Giles's words.

Anya glared at him. "I'm making an analogy here. As in letting the cat out of the bag? Get it?"

"Oh."

"Maybe if you guys stopped griping at each other, Giles could actually answer," Dawn said without taking her gaze from the sling she was now carefully winding around Buffy's shoulder and broken arm.

Anya flushed slightly, then looked at Giles. The librarian raised an eyebrow, then restarted where she'd interrupted him. "The first thing we do is cast a boundary spell," he told them. "It's far too risky to believe that we can keep Tara's spirit imprisoned in something as fragile as a piece of crystal when, as Anya pointed out, a single crack would free her."

"So can't we just convince her to stay?" Xander asked. "In the interest of helping Willow and all that happy-sappy?"

Giles shook his head. "That's unlikely. Since her appearance, even though Tara has been visible to everyone, she's been seen nowhere out of range of Willow. It's obvious Willow is the reason her spirit is earthbound to begin with. Released from the jar, her spirit will head right back to where she belongs—at Willow's side."

"Let me see if I understand this," Xander said. "This boundary spell will keep Tara in the Magic Box. But . . ." He hesitated. "But will it keep Willow out?"

"No," Giles said. "Which is why we need to perform it immediately."

"I don't get it," Xander began. "If she—"

"I'll explain fully after the spell is complete. For the safety of us all, it *must* be done before Willow gets here." Giles lifted one eyebrow. "And you can bet it won't be long until she notices Tara's absence."

"All right," Anya said firmly. "Tell me what you need." She frowned. "I hope we have all the ingredients in stock. There's been a run lately on—"

Giles held up a hand. "I'm sure you do. Simple stuff—purified sand, three yellow candles, and two white ones. The hardest item will be a twig from a weeping willow tree used to hang a witch."

Anya looked dismayed for a moment, then her expression cleared. "Wait—I think I do have one of those. Very expensive, had to have it shipped all the way from southeast England." Her eyes darkened and she gave Giles a sidelong glance. "Say, you aren't going to burn it, are you? I can't sell the thing if it's damaged."

"No burning," the former Watcher assured her. "I promise."

"All right," she said, but Anya didn't look particularly convinced. Even so, she came up with the candles and sand Giles had requested, then reluctantly retrieved the coveted piece of willow tree and held it out. That done, the librarian knelt and carefully poured the purified sand into a small, rough pentagram shape just inside the shop's front door with the candles at each point. Finally he lit the waiting candles and crouched over them with the crystal jar cradled in one hand and the willow twig in the other.

"By these runes," he intoned as he used the tip of the twig to draw two shapes into the sand, *"I bind thee, Tara, to me and to this place."* One shape represented possession, but the other, Anya knew, was the symbol for travel. It seemed so much to be the opposite of what they were looking for that she was opening her mouth to question it when Giles drew a firm horizontal line, completely bisecting the second rune. Then he wrote Tara's name in the sand, added a rune symbol that represented a man and wrote his own name next to that, finally etching a circle around the entire thing.

They'd all been waiting and watching, and it all seemed so . . . *placid* and uneventful that it completely caught them by surprise when every last light in the Magic Shop building flickered and went out.

"Uh . . . ," Xander began.

"Shhhh!" Anya said as she poked him with the sharp tip of her finger. She tucked her hands under her arms as the temperature of the air suddenly dropped by a startling twenty degrees.

Giles's next words raised more goosebumps. *"Without my consent,"* he continued, *"never will you be free of this building. And should I die by any hand other than the natural laws of the universe, you will be bound to the very bones of my body unto ash in their final resting place."*

And finally, to close the spell, he pried loose the top of the teardrop jar and poured the milky-looking essence of Tara within the circle he'd drawn. Circles within circles, and all designed to bind in this world, and beyond.

Tara's spirit expanded in a ball shape, luminescent and filled with light, and spun slowly. Then it rose, faster and faster and faster, until it hit the ceiling and exploded over them, expanded in all directions against the room's upper boundary like a thin layer of golden, living cloud. It covered the ceiling in the time it took to blink, then it began to whirl, rolling itself outward until only a three-foot piece of it, thicker and more substantial-looking than before, remained. That piece gained speed, suddenly whizzing around the room faster than any of the Scooby gang could follow it, trying desperately to find an escape route.

"Giles?" Dawn sounded frightened as she jerked one way, then another, and tried to keep pace with the spirit's frantic movement. "Giles, what's wrong with her? Is she in pain?"

The former Watcher shook his head and calmly blew out the candles one by one, then carefully swiped his hand across the surface of the sand, obliterating the written remains of his spell. "No. I imagine she's doing what any of us would do if we opened our eyes to find ourselves imprisoned somewhere—trying to find a way out."

While the spiritual essence zinging around them was clearly making Dawn nervous, Anya was more concerned with Giles. "*'Bones of my body'?* I guess you woke up on the morbid side of the bed this morning."

"Yeah," Xander agreed. "What's up with that?"

Dawn had done a passable job on the arm sling and now Buffy was leaning back on her chair, resting as her gaze followed the passage of Tara's spirit around the room. "I think I understand why he worded it that way," she said quietly.

"I never said I didn't understand it," Anya said smartly. "It's just . . . macabre to hear it out loud."

Dawn scowled. "Willow wouldn't kill Giles," she said loudly. When they looked at her, she lowered her voice with effort. "I mean, she's had her chance to put the permanent check-out on all of us at one time or the other lately, and she hasn't."

Xander rolled his eyes. "I guess you haven't been paying attention, 'cause it sure wasn't for lack of trying."

Dawn opened her mouth to argue, but Giles held up his hand. "Xander's right," he said.

"Doesn't happen often," Anya muttered, but there was no real meanness in her voice, so Xander just grinned a little.

"Tara's influence has been the only controlling factor in Willow's behavior," Giles told them. "Not only do we have no guarantee that this will continue to be the case, we can't count on the fact that on her own, Tara's spirit could or would leave Willow's loft."

"It was outside," Buffy said. "That's where I first saw it."

"True," Giles agreed. "But again—no guarantees. Once Willow realizes that Tara's spirit has been taken, it's highly probable that she's going to panic and do whatever it takes to get Tara back. When she finds out that we're the ones who have Tara—and she will, you can count on that—based on her recent attitude, she's going to be very, *very* angry."

Xander looked thoughtful. "So by saying that if you die by . . . what was it?"

"Anything other than natural causes," Anya filled in.

"Yeah," Xander said. "So if she has any ideas about, uh, losing her temper—"

"Oh, just say it," Anya said crankily. "If she kills Giles."

Xander swallowed. "Right. If she does, she won't ever get Tara back."

"Exactly," Giles said. His expression was grave. "I do want you all to remember that while this will protect me, it might not keep her from harming the rest of you."

"Sounds like the makings of a stand-off to me," Buffy said. Her voice was gaining strength, but it was clear she needed some sleep and some healing time. "Willow says 'Okay, I'm going to kill—fill in the blank here—unless you give me Tara back.' You say, 'If you do, I'll never release her.' What then?"

Giles looked unhappy. "I'm not sure," he admitted. "I did the best I could with the spell available. The wording guarantees that murdering the originator of the spell won't free the spirit. Alas, the binding spell won't allow me to tie Tara's essence to more than one person. I could try to alter the spell, but there's a good chance I would destroy it."

Buffy sat up straighter. "Wait—destroy what? The spell, or Tara?"

"Her spirit, yes."

Buffy sank bank against the chair. "Then we do the best we can to stay safe." She looked at Anya. "A few protection charms wouldn't hurt, I'll bet."

Anya nodded. "I'm on it. Charms all around."

During the course of their conversation, the frantic pace of the ghostly essence had slowed and finally stopped. Now it hung in the corner, floating and swirling like a mini-tornado. As Anya worked behind the counter, gathering up the ingredients for the protection amulets, eventually even the spirit's restless eddying slowed and came to a stop. They watched and waited, and finally the image of Tara bled through the mist until it was recognizable. For a long while, it said nothing, then—

"Let me go, Giles. I must return to Willow. I belong with her."

The spirit's voice was soft and full of pain and longing, and the sound of it sent a shiver up Giles's spine. "I'm sorry, Tara. I can't do that."

"Tara," she whispered. *"It's been so long since anyone called me that."*

Frowning, Anya stared at the ghost. "Why? I mean, that's your name—"

"Willow does not think of me as Tara," the spirit

said hollowly. *"I can hear her thoughts, see into her heart. She thinks of me only as 'the Ghost of Tara.' To her, I'm not quite real, not all of what she wants. In time—a very short time—all of you will realize the same thing."* The spirit paused, then turned her see-through gaze to Giles. *"You should let me return to her,"* she told him. *"You think that you can control her by controlling me, but you're wrong."*

"We have to try." Listening to her, Giles thought he could already understand why Willow couldn't quite accept this spiritual entity as a substitute for her dead lover. It *was* Tara, of that there was no doubt. But it also *wasn't*—there was a formality about it, a stiffness that spoke of a barrier between life and death that could not be crossed, even with love.

"No," Buffy said. "Giles, I think we're wrong. I mean, we don't want to *control* Willow, do we?" She looked at the librarian and the rest of them. "What we want is to . . . I don't know. *Save* her. Right?"

The Ghost of Tara drifted over to stand in front of Buffy, making the Slayer shift uncomfortably. *"You cannot force salvation on Willow, Buffy. She must find it herself or perish."*

Xander rubbed his eyes. "Did I really just hear a ghost say the word 'perish'?"

Tara's spirit turned toward him and for a moment her eyes blazed. *"Do you think this is funny, Xander?"* She gestured at herself and then spun with her arms spread, like a model showing off her outfit on an elevated runway. With a start they all realized she was still clothed in the top and jeans in which she'd died. They could see a splattering of blood across the front of her blouse, but when her back was turned, the image was much more horrifying—there the scarlet stain of Tara's death had spread across the fabric of her blouse, soaking into it for eternity and dripping down to coat the waistband of her jeans. The red pattern glistened wetly in the soft light of the Magic Box, a horrifying reminder of exactly how Tara's physical self had died. Buffy winced and wondered what it was doing to Willow's mind to see this every time the Ghost of Tara appeared in front of her. The mental anguish her long-time friend was enduring had to be staggering, unimaginable.

"N-no," Xander stuttered. "Of course not. I just meant—"

But the Ghost of Tara cut him off. *"You joke and try to find humor in everything, and the rest of you go along with it because not one of you has a clue what else to do. You deal with Willow the best way you know how, and while that has always worked in the past, trust me when I say that if you—if all of you—had any idea of what's coming, the very last thing you'd be doing now is laughing."*

"Oh, dear," Anya said unhappily. "I really hate it when ghosts start prophesying. Trust me—they *never* tell the living about anything good."

Giles scowled and folded his arms. "Then perhaps you'd care to enlighten us about the future," he suggested, "since it appears you have a heads-up on things." He and the others waited expectantly.

But for now, the Ghost of Tara would say no more.

Chapter Twenty

Willow was going to have to do the clean-up inch by painful inch.

She started with her Wiccans.

Njeri and Anan were dead, killed by the creature of her own making. She hoped it had been quick and that neither had suffered, but she couldn't know for sure. Amy and seven others had been badly beaten by the golem. Even Ena, whom Willow had last seen headed toward Buffy in fury, had gone down not long after Buffy had thrown herself out the window. Running on anger and adrenaline, it had taken the crash and spray of flying glass across her face to make Ena realize just how badly she was already injured and that she simply didn't have the energy to go after the Slayer. Standing in front of the shattered window, she'd finally turned back to Willow as if to apologize . . . then collapsed.

It was hard for Willow to focus on exactly what she was feeling as she surveyed the wreckage—*again*—of what had until recently been her own little kingdom. The corpses, the injured, the destruction—it was all overwhelming, so much so that apparently even the Ghost of Tara had decided to bow out of the scene for now. And why not? What would Tara's spirit have to listen to but Willow's infuriated ranting and the venomous promises of revenge that Willow couldn't seem to stop from pouring out of her own mouth.

"She'll pay, oh, you can bet she will," she hissed as she struggled through the backbreaking labor of clearing away the debris just so she could get to Njeri's and Anan's bodies. She couldn't even use magicks to clean this up; the deaths of these two women and all the efforts that had been expended by herself and the others, injured and uninjured, to fight the golem had completely sapped her, left her as tired out and used-up as a dead cactus in the middle of the Mojave. She would recover, of course, but for now, thanks once more to Buffy and Giles and the rest of those little wannabe do-gooders, she would have to clean up this mess with her own two flesh and blood hands.

But first . . . she would have to prepare the bodies for . . . burial.

Willow pressed her lips together as she realized she'd almost used the word "disposal." Had she really gotten that cold toward others, so uncaring that although they'd fought for her and supplied her with their own power, she thought of their lifeless bodies as nothing more than trash that she had to take care of?

She hoped not—she might be all business and she certainly was focused, but that was a little too far afield on the icy mental ocean than even she wanted to travel. And because of that, maybe it was a good thing that she would have to take care of Njeri and Anan herself, touch them and ready them and *feel* them as she sent their shells to their final resting. There were also, she realized, other things she ought to be keeping in mind, like the women she'd pressed into serving her and who, on way too many accounts, had given their all in doing so.

"What are you going to do with their bodies?"

Willow didn't look at Amy as the other woman sidled up to her, and she squashed the urge to lash out. There was a tone in Amy's voice that she didn't like, a conspiratorial nastiness that for some reason she didn't want to associate with herself. Yes, she was the Big Bad around Sunnydale now—or, she thought bitterly, at least as much as her own creations would allow her to be—but there was still something intrinsic in her soul that made her not want to be thought of as a criminal. That, she decided, was the tone of Amy's voice: criminal. There was some fine line in there, an almost indiscernible difference between evil and criminal. Evil had *potential*—it could be grand and sweeping and powerful, beautiful in its own darkness. It had designs, always aiming for something bigger and better. Criminal was just dirty and petty and, for someone like her, completely unworthy of her time.

"We will wash them, and dress them, and treat them with respect," Willow said stiffly. "Then I'll cremate them." The way she wanted to do it would require a solid dose of power and first she would have to wait for her energy to rebuild, but Amy didn't have to know that. It wouldn't take long—she was already starting to feel recharged, like a cold car battery warming in the sun.

"Cremate them, huh? À la Warren?"

Willow whirled and Amy took an automatic step backward. "No, *not* like that! Not at all—and don't you *ever* say that name around me again!" She was suddenly furious all over again. "We'll have a ceremony and mourn their passing the way we should!"

"Sorry," Amy said quickly. "Really—I didn't mean to upset you. I'll—I'll just help. Whatever you want me to do, you just tell me." She nodded to reinforce her words. "Anything at all."

Gritting her teeth, Willow inhaled hard through her nose and tried to calm herself. A show of temper right now would not be a good thing, just a useless waste of power and time. "Fine."

It took the two of them, plus Ellen and Chiwa, a good two hours to get everyone patched up to where the women stopped their moaning and decided they were going to live. Ellen and Chiwa had somehow escaped injury, and Willow thought it was a pretty safe bet that both had hid—Ellen was one of the least powerful Wiccans and the one on whom Willow had nearly focused her anger when the remaining members of her coven had questioned her loyalty after the *sine kot diabl*'s destruction. From the way the woman looked now, Willow doubted there was going to be a repeat of that old argument, and it was clear that she and Chiwa—neither had a scratch on them—had simply made themselves scarce during the battle. Willow could almost understand Chiwa's fear, since the woman had come back from whatever hell to which Giles had banished her, but Ellen . . . there was no word for it but cowardice. Willow was going to have to live with that, because beating a cowardly dog didn't do anything but make it even more afraid.

There were a lot of injuries, some nastier than others. Wounds that Willow herself had sustained in battle or wounds she had inflicted upon others—such as the miserable burns she'd given Njeri early on when the woman had questioned her power—were easy to heal. The barest thought, the passing of her hand, and *voila*—all gone. But the golem's damage to her coven members was not so easily repaired; it seemed like eons ago that she had walked into the sterile environment of a hospital surgery room and pulled Warren's bullet from Buffy's body by sheer force of will, then repaired the fragile flesh ripped apart by the passage of that tiny, misshapen piece of metal. The broken bones and battered bodies of tonight's war—and there were many—would mostly have to heal on their own.

It took everything Willow had to concentrate on the purification ritual for Njeri and Anan. While the other women rested, she, Amy, Chiwa, and Ellen stripped the corpses and carefully washed them from head to toe, then rubbed each with warmed Sabbat oil to which she'd added one part each of galangal, vervain, and lavender in order to strengthen the mixture.

Soon, however, the scent of the oil filled the loft and calmed everyone in it. Willow found herself moving a little slower, putting more thought into each stroke of the soft cloth as she considered the loss of life before her and wondered how each young woman's family would handle the disappearance. With the exception of Amy, she really didn't know much about these young women, nor did she care to . . . or at least that's how it had been in the past. Now, however, with two of them lying dead on a table before her, having been bathed and redressed in filmy white dresses for their fiery burials, she couldn't help but wonder. Anan had been in love with Flo, but that didn't preclude the existence of a mother and father, perhaps siblings or other family members. Njeri had been full of passion and fire—had there been a boyfriend in her life, someone who had missed the lovely young black woman's company all these nights and been the root of her resentfulness toward Willow and her forced participation in Willow's little power coven? Willow would probably never know.

Over by the fireplace, even Oz had finally calmed down, or perhaps it was just exhaustion from the hours of snapping and snarling post-battle. For a change, even Spike seemed fairly lucid; he had stopped his rocking and crying, and although he still mumbled to himself every twenty or thirty seconds, his eyes were clearer than they had been since Willow had brought him here from the demon's cave. Maybe the guilt-soaked parts of his brain were finally wringing themselves out.

She had positioned the deceased young women next to each other but at opposites—one's head next to the other's feet—and now she readied a large white candle for each, placing it on the table a few inches above their heads. The final step was to light a stick of sweet incense at the four corners and the two center side points of the table. When the time came, the flame of each candle would bounce from itself to the stick of incense closest to it, and from that one to the next. Ultimately the bodies would be encased in a rectangle of light and scent, and from there . . .

Willow picked up her *Book of Shadows*, then ran her hand across its ill-used cover. Only its binding to herself had kept it from being sucked through the portal Giles had opened during the first spell he'd enacted. "We're ready to do the passing rite," she announced. "Make a circle."

The rest of her coven made their way to the table, some more slowly than others. It would be a long time before bodies were healed and her coven was back to normal—if it ever happened at all. She could find replacements for Njeri and Anan, but repairing the spirits and rebuilding the trust of the remaining Wiccans was something else entirely. When everyone was in position, she flipped the *Book of Shadows* open to the pages she'd already marked.

"Wise Queen of the Dark," she read slowly, "pierce the veil before our eyes. We have lost our sisters, and turn in pain and regret to thee. By the stars above and the earth below, you who know the truths of Life and Death, pray with us as we perform our sacred rite." Willow raised her gaze from the words and glanced at the candle placed above Njeri's head. Its wick blazed to life in a thin column at least four inches high, then it settled back down and burned normally.

"Lord of the Wise and Dark," Willow continued, "pierce the veil before our eyes. We have heard the funereal knell and wait to hear what thee can tell. Two we treasure have passed away, and of Death you know the secret spells. Lend us comfort here this night, and be with us in our sacred rites."

Another glance, this time at the candle positioned above Anan's head. Fire bloomed on its tip and, like the other one, rose high in the air before withering to a regular flame. The air in the loft cooled noticeably and the heat eddying off the two candles and the burning incense sticks took on visible form as feathery smoke began to weave from burning tip to burning tip, forming a lacy veil above the two bodies.

"Our sisters have passed your Gate," Willow chanted. "While we may well question the hand of Fate, we ask your blessing on them. Help speed their journey and receive them with love in thy heart. By the earth below and the stars above, cradle them in forever peace and love."

Willow closed the book and waved her hand in the air. The candle flames jumped again, blazing high. "These flames we light to guide their way, their joining to commit their earthly bodies to you forever. When it's done, their journey ends." She brought her hand down in a sharp swipe and the flame on each candle arced in opposite directions, bouncing to the nearest stick of incense, then along the next two, until each found its way to the opposite candle. In an instant the bodies were within a floating rectangle of flame, their pale, lifeless faces washed in the buttery glow of the candlelight.

"A moment of meditation," Willow said softly, "to say good-bye." She bowed her head and the others did the same, but she didn't let them have long. A mere five seconds later she raised her face again. "Rest well," she said simply, and gave a sharp snap of her fingers.

The formation of candlelight spread and reformed into a rolling oval of flame that covered the tabletop and obliterated the remains of Njeri and Anan.

It took three minutes. The flames went out as suddenly as they'd started, leaving nothing—not even a bit of ash or charred piece of fabric—behind. In an unbidden and unwanted comparison, Willow realized that the ending of this *was* very much like Warren's had been: a flash of flame and then . . . nothing. With him it had been a hollow victory, revenge on the one hand, but on the other, as though the man had never existed.

Well . . . not really.

Willow's pain and loss lived on. Would the women gathered here tonight forget more easily?

"What have you done?"

Willow whirled at the unfamiliar voice, then her mouth fell open as she realized that Flo—a lucid, vocal, healed, and apparently sane Flo—was standing only a few feet away. "Flo! You're—"

"Awake?" Flo's gaze raked her as sharply as a pair of claws. "Whole? Oh, yes." She stepped around Willow and went up to the table. There was nothing there, but when Flo pressed her hand against the wood on which Anan had lain a short while ago, Willow knew Flo could feel the lingering heat of the magickal cremation. "I heard everything, you know." Flo stared at the table as if mesmerized. "The passing rite. The battle." She raised her haunted gaze to meet Willow's. "Even the exact moment when that creature you created killed her."

Willow swallowed, not knowing what to say. So much of this was spinning out of her control—the golem, the loss of life, even the fact that Flo was up and walking and talking. The sleep spell she'd put on Flo should have kept her comatose literally until Willow herself was dead or she was entirely healed. While it was certainly a testament to the untapped depths of her own power, Willow had never expected it to work so quickly.

"Finish it," Flo said softly. "You have to do the closing rite or it's not complete."

Willow nodded, watching the other woman warily along with the remainder of the coven. Flo didn't say anything else, just joined the circle around the table to where she would have been directly beside Anan. Flo's sudden waking had rattled Willow more than she cared to admit, and now she inhaled quietly, mentally commanding her racing heartbeat to go back to normal. For the ceremony she had donned a velvet robe, deep purple in respect for the dead, and now she felt overheated by the heavy fabric, almost light-headed. Damn it, she *would* finish this, and so what if Flo's appearance had brought an unexpected addition to the ritual? It *would* be done.

Lifting her chin, Willow reached into one of her pockets and pulled out a small silver bell engraved with sacred symbols. She held it high, then gave it three gentle rings. Without having to be told, all of the Wiccans turned and faced south.

"The bell tolls for Njeri and Anan," Willow said in a clear, loud voice. "They stand before the portals to the lands beyond death, prepared to experience the mysteries. We ask that you greet and comfort our sisters as they enter."

They all turned back to the table and waited. From an elaborately painted box at her feet, Willow withdrew two carefully folded packets of clothes, the tattered remains of everything the dead women had been wearing, all heavily stained with blood. After placing the packets in the center of the table, she extended her closed fists toward the material. The rest of the coven did the same.

"Keeper of the knowledge of death," Willow said softly, "open the gates for our sisters and let them enter through the gates by which all must pass. Remove the sorrow that binds them to our world and show them the way." As one, they all turned their fists and extended their fingers. On their open palms glowed tiny orange flames.

"We part with regret—"

"And love," Flo whispered.

"—and love," Willow added. "And with that same love and no regret shall we someday meet again." She hesitated, then nodded at Flo. If the other woman knew the rite, Willow would allow her to finish the ceremony.

Flo closed her eyes for a moment, then opened them and stared at the bloody mementos on the table. "In our memories," she said, "and in our hearts we will recall the most precious moments shared with Anan and Njeri. In our hearts will we find their faces and their love, and it is those things that will bring us closer to them." The sound of her voice turned hoarse and Flo paused; it was obvious she was fighting to continue without having her words break. "So let us not mourn them," she managed after clearing her throat. "Let us instead have comfort in their ascension. And each day, as we see the sun sink into the horizon at the end of the evening and rise at the beginning of the morning, let us have comfort. Each year, as the leaves wither in autumn and return in spring, let us have comfort."

Flo glanced at Willow and the others and nodded. Each of the women gave a small push in the air and the flames on their palms floated away and hovered just above the two piles of fabric. "You are freed from the shells of your bodies," Flo said quietly. "Now you can walk without fear in the realm of death. Now you can journey in your dreams, and revel in your emotions. Join with the Universe and gather your will and strength to be reborn. Death is only the beginning of life."

And as the last of her words dissipated on the cool air currents, the small ball of fire above the table spread into a dome and sank slowly over the packets of fabric, finally consuming the last of the earthly evidence of Njeri's and Anan's involvement with Willow's coven.

Chapter Twenty-One

"We need to discuss what happened at Willow's," Giles said.

Looking back at him was a sad and sorry bunch, indeed. Bruised, battered, and broken, Buffy and the rest of the gang nevertheless waited expectantly for his next words.

Anya squared her shoulders and was brave enough to speak up first. "All right. I can discuss. Let's start with the fact that in an all-for-one and one-for-all sense, we lost." She looked at the others but no one disagreed.

"The fight isn't the only thing we lost," Buffy said gravely.

Xander was sitting on one of the chairs and had his elbows on his knees. His hands were clasped and all he could do was stare at the floor. "Yeah," he said in a thick voice. "Two people . . . dead. Man, I just can't believe we did that."

Anya scowled at him. "What's this 'we' stuff?" she demanded. "I didn't kill anyone, and neither did you. It was that golem thing, and that was Willow's own fault."

"No," said Buffy. "It's my fault."

"All right, it's your fault," Anya agreed.

"Buffy, don't be so hard on yourself," Dawn said. "You had no idea something this horrible would happen."

But Buffy shook her head. "Come on, how long have I been around all things supernatural? Common sense should have made me work out in advance what I told Riley to do."

Giles took off his glasses and cleaned them furiously. "Surely I don't need to remind you that the golem was *not* Riley, but a manifestation of him—a . . . puppet, if you will, with only the barest of his essence trapped inside it."

"Kind of like how you have Tara trapped here," Dawn suggested.

Giles slipped his glasses back on and considered that. "No," he said after a moment. "Not at all. The spirit of Tara that's with us here in the Magic Shop is a more . . . *complete* rendition of Tara than the golem ever was of Riley. And even here, the Ghost of Tara isn't quite right; there is an essential sense of soul, or whatever you want to call it, that's most definitely and noticeably missing."

Buffy stood, wincing as her injured arm bounced

against her body. "If you're saying that makes me blameless, it falls flat."

Giles sighed. "I will allow that you could have worded your instructions to the creature a bit more clearly. On the other hand, you're not a sorceress or a Wiccan, and your strength is not in knowing such things."

Buffy rolled her eyes. "Great. So under all the Britishisms, what you're really saying is that I'm the brawn, not the brains."

Giles blinked. "That's a rather harsh way of putting it."

Buffy shrugged. "Reality is a harsh thing. If you don't think so, just remember the body count."

"It wasn't like you meant for it to happen," Dawn put in. "It was an accident."

"That doesn't make it all right," Buffy shot back. She ground her teeth as she realized she was echoing exactly what Willow had told her in the loft.

"Well, you can't bring them back," Anya said. "Beating yourself up over it is senseless and a waste of time."

"We can always count on Anya for bluntness," Xander muttered.

Giles rubbed the back of his neck, trying to relieve the tension in his muscles. "The words might not be pretty, but the wisdom is there nonetheless," he said. "If we could bring them—or anyone—back, we wouldn't be in this situation now."

"Look," Anya said. "You guys need to figure out exactly what you're doing. I mean, you just keep going over and getting your—excuse me, *our*—asses solidly kicked, and for what?"

"To stop Willow," Dawn said.

"Great," Anya said. "To stop her from doing *what*?"

For a long moment, no one answered—no one knew how to. When the answer came, it was from the one among them they'd least expected to supply it.

"Stop her from amassing any more power."

They all jumped. They just weren't used to the Ghost of Tara being there yet, the way she'd suddenly appear out of nowhere and join the conversation, the way she'd fade from sight if she decided she was through talking. She never really left, of course—she couldn't—but since Giles had released her from the jar, she'd remained out of sight a good deal of the time.

That statement, at least, got the conversation going again.

"Yeah," Buffy said. "She's already packing way more punch than any self-respecting witch ought to be. We definitely need to pull the plug on the celestial battery."

"Or at least flip the charger to low," Xander put in. "The way she's running now, she's beginning to remind me of a Wiccan version of the Borg."

"And she's got to let Oz and Spike go, too," Dawn said.

"She won't."

"Well, why not?" Anya came forward and stared at the Ghost of Tara. "What use are they to her?"

"They give her companionship," Tara's spirit said.

"And whether she realizes it or not, they're her ties to the world she left behind after she killed Warren."

"Well, hey, she could just let 'em go and come on back," Xander said, finally abandoning his study of the worn floorboards. "We have this thing around here that's called forgive and forget." When no one said anything, a corner of his mouth twisted. "Okay, so maybe it's forgive and not forget. Whatever. She could still come back."

"Willow doesn't want to come back."

Giles tilted his head. "Then what *does* she want? If she's amassing all this power, it must be for a purpose." He glanced at Buffy. "If she's still talking about revenge on Jonathan and Andrew, I'm afraid that's out of the question."

The Ghost of Tara's eyes glittered. *"She wants me."*

"But she has you," Dawn pointed out. "I mean, we only kidnapped . . . er, ghost-napped—whatever."

"A trade, then," Giles said. "She must relinquish the power she's been amassing in order for us to return you."

The spirit looked away. *"She will never agree to that,"* the Ghost of Tara finally said. *"At best, as Dawn suggested, she might return Spike and Oz. But no more than that."*

Anya frowned. "But she loves you. I don't understand."

"I've told you before, and you've all noticed it on your own. This"—the spirit waved a hand at her own ghostly image—*"isn't me, at least not the me that Willow wants."*

Xander frowned. "I don't get it."

"Oh," Buffy suddenly said in a small, surprised voice. "Oh my God."

Xander jerked. "What?" he demanded.

Buffy looked from the Ghost of Tara to Giles. "I understand now—she wants to bring Tara back. The *real* Tara. Tara in-the-flesh-and-with-real-blood kind." For a stunned second, she looked absolutely shell-shocked, then she stared at the spirit. "My God, we've done everything we can, over and over, to stop her when we didn't even realize that all she wanted in the world was to bring you back!" She swallowed against a sudden feeling of nausea. "People have *died* because of this, because we thought Willow was doing something evil."

"That's all great and dandy, but let's not forget that Willow wasn't exactly the Sunnydale fairy godmother in her great quest to make this happen," Anya said sharply. "I think raising head-chomping, energy-sucking cats and destruction man-shaped mounds of mud qualifies as evil." She tapped herself on the top of the head. "Very narrow brush with toothy death, remember?"

"Wait a sec—did you say what I think I heard you say?" Dawn had been sitting on the floor with her back against the wall, and now she sat up straight as her sister's words sank in, turning her attention to the spirit as well. "Willow's going to try to bring Tara back from the dead, like she did Buffy?"

The Ghost of Tara nodded.

Xander looked from Giles to Anya. "Can she do that? I mean, why not? She did it to Buffy—"

Anya shook her head. "No way. Wrong kind of death. She"—Anya pointed at the specter—"died by man's hand, totally of this earth and all that. Buffy's death was all mystical. Two completely different realms."

"*She won't accept that.*"

Giles stared into space for a few moments, thinking. "Are you absolutely sure it can't be done?" he finally asked. "Is there any possibility at all that she'll be able to—"

"*No.*"

Giles pressed his lips together.

Buffy looked from Giles to Anya to the Ghost of Tara. "So in the end, it doesn't matter. All we did was delay the final result."

"Well," Xander said, a bit too lightly. "End of discussion, right?"

"*She won't accept that,*" the Ghost of Tara repeated.

Xander frowned and looked at the spirit. No one spoke for a long time, then Dawn finally said, "She's going to be very, very angry when she fails, isn't she?"

The Ghost of Tara didn't answer. She didn't have to.

Epilogue

"**G**o home," Willow told them. "All of you. Rest and tend to your wounds. Come back in a week and I'll find replacements for . . ." She hesitated. Careful here with the wording. "For the open slots. Then we'll see where we stand, and what we need to do to perform the resurrection spell so that you can all return to your normal lives."

"Our normal lives?" Flo's soft voice floated above the heads of the other women seated around the loft. She was standing off to the side, away from the others, still dressed in the shimmering blue gown she had worn while comatose. The long ribbons still dangled from her hair and she looked like some kind of haunted, dark-haired fairy. "What is left of our lives now that you have forced us to live yours?"

"Things haven't changed that much," Willow said

shortly, although the instant the words left her mouth, she wished she could pluck them from the air and stuff them back into her own throat. How ridiculous— "haven't changed?" Two women were dead, others were missing and might as well be after having been banished to parts unknown, the remainder beaten and scarred. God, she was tired—way too much so to argue about things.

"I dreamed, you know," Flo said. Her eyes were hazy, as though she were looking at something the rest of them couldn't see. "While I was sleeping. I dreamed, over and over, that I was back in the place where that Watcher sent me. I had constant nightmares from which I could not escape because at least in life, in reality, I might have had a chance to someday get away. To win." Her gaze bored into Willow's from across the room. "But in the kind of sleep you put me, it was like death. And in death—*from* death—there is no escape."

A chill ran across Willow's shoulders. Everyday life and the struggles that came with it were bad enough—maybe even worse in the grand, supernatural-infested town of Sunnydale—but the idea of being trapped in your own dream state while fighting for your life . . . that was just unspeakable. The Ghost of Tara had told her that dropping Flo into a fugue state would give her peace, and it had never occurred to Willow that the spirit could be wrong about anything.

Speaking of, where *was* the Ghost of Tara, any-way? Willow hadn't seen her or felt her presence since the height of her battle with the golem. Strange—the

Ghost of Tara had been a nearly constant companion, at her side nearly every waking moment since her first appearance. Her absence now put a sliver of fear into Willow's heart, but she refused to dwell on that right now, would not let herself consider that it was anything more than temporary. She would be back. Willow was sure of it.

"Go home," Willow said again. She couldn't keep the bitterness from bleeding into her voice and she wasn't going to bother trying. Her Wiccans didn't need to be told a third time, and she watched them file down the stairs in silence. Over the coming days she would need to find her coven's replacements and repair the damage to the loft, and she would think carefully indeed before her next move.

So far everything she'd done had backfired on her . . . well, everything except killing Warren. Funny how that was probably the most brutal, yet no one had come looking for retribution for it . . . and wasn't that just an indication that the murderer had deserved what he'd received? After that she'd tried a method to get power, then made a protection creature, and both had failed her. And that last one . . . her disappointment in the golem was almost suffocating. Pulled from the earth to protect her and hers, the being had not only turned on her, but blithely demolished the coven she had so carefully assembled to help her exist safely in this worthless little town. In retrospect, when she had pulled the golem from the earth, perhaps she should have allowed her other Wiccans to help here, thereby strengthening the golem's bond to *all* of them. But it was too late for recriminations and second thoughts; now Willow could only try to learn from her mistakes and move on.

Standing in the silence of the abandoned loft, Willow surveyed the damage and decided that things were going to change, oh yes. She would put all her energies into finalizing what was needed to bring Tara back—the power sources, the proper words to modify the spell, anything and everything that was necessary to accomplish her goal.

As for the Slayer, Giles, and the rest of that annoying little group, they were going to learn, once and for all, that the Willow they'd once known no longer existed. Now they were *targets,* and it made no difference to her that some were human and some were demon, or even that one was supposedly "chosen." Willow would consider carefully the high prices that Buffy and the others would pay for crossing her, for destroying her coven, and for stealing the loyalty of the golem. Willow could turn her back on many things, but this time they had humiliated her, diminished her in the eyes of her Wiccan underlings and made her own coven mistrustful of her. This time they had killed. They needed to learn that the woman who would have once forgiven them was gone, left behind along another path of their lives.

Now the Willow who was left walked alone. And she would show no mercy to those who stood in the way of resurrecting Tara.

ABOUT THE AUTHOR

Yvonne Navarro spent her youth (which is ongoing) making up stuff. When she "grew up" she started writing more and more, and now she's had nearly a hundred stories and over a dozen books published. She's even managed to get a few cool awards (most recently the Bram Stoker award for *Buffy the Vampire Slayer: The Willow Files, Vol. 2*). She has no spare time, that stuff having been stolen away by various evil entities in her life, such as husband Weston (acquired in 2002) and a deaf Great Dane (another creature with an ongoing youth) called Chili Lily Beast. She finally moved to southern Arizona in 2002 and is now secretly trying to figure out how to raise the temperature of the high desert surrounding her home by about fifteen degrees. Yvonne maintains a big old Web site at www.yvonnenavarro.com with all kinds of fun stuff on it. She's also the owner of a little online bookstore called Dusty Stacks (www.dustystacks.com). Come visit!

"Witches can't be allowed to alter the fabric of life that way, for selfish reasons. We'd manipulate the world until it came unglued. . . ." —Tara, "Forever"

The Ghost of Tara has disappeared. At first Willow thought it was because of something she'd done—or worse, that the universe was again conspiring to hurt her. But it's almost impossible to keep secrets from a witch, especially one as powerful as Willow, and ultimately she learns that Buffy and the gang are the culprits.

Willow desperately wants Tara back. Not only does she miss her immensely, the spirit's presence is necessary to perform the resurrection ritual Willow's been working on. Though her first impulse is to charge off and bring her wrath down upon the heads of her old friends, her coven reminds her that in the past, when Willow has allowed anger to control her, she has failed. Willow must develop an alternate plan to regain Tara's spirit and perform the ritual.

Buffy and the Scoobies hope to drain Willow's power, and release Spike and Oz from their enslavement. But Willow's anger is endless, and it seems she'll stop at nothing in her fight to bring Tara back, no matter what the cost. . . .

Wicked Willow III
Broken Sunrise

The final installment of a new alternate-history trilogy
by Bram Stoker–winner Yvonne Navarro
Based on the hit TV series created by Joss Whedon

Available September 2004
From Simon Spotlight Entertainment
Published by Simon & Schuster

As many as 1 in 3 Americans
who have HIV... don't know it.

TAKE CONTROL.
KNOW YOUR STATUS.
GET TESTED.

To learn more about HIV testing,
or get a free guide to HIV and
other sexually transmitted diseases:

www.knowhivaids.org
1-866-344-KNOW

Everyone's got his demons....

ANGEL™

If it takes an eternity, he will make amends.

Original stories based
on the TV show
Created by Joss Whedon
& David Greenwalt

Published by Simon & Schuster

2311-01

Buffy the Vampire Slayer can toss a one-liner more lethal than her right hook—without breaking a sweat. Now fans of Buffy's wicked wordplay won't want to miss this exhaustive collection of the funniest, most telling, and often poignant quotes from the Emmy-nominated television show.

"'Her abuse of the English language is such that I understand only every other sentence. . . .'" —Wesley Wyndham-Pryce (quoting Giles) on Buffy, "Bad Girls"

Categorized and complete with a color-photo insert, this notable quote compendium will have you eagerly enhancing your Buffy-speak.

"If I had the Slayer's power, I'd be punning right about now." —Buffy Summers, "Helpless"

Buffy the vampire slayer™

THE QUOTABLE SLAYER
The last word on life, love, and lingo in the Buffy-verse!

Compiled by Micol Ostow and Steven Brezenoff

AVAILABLE DECEMBER 2003 FROM SIMON PULSE